NOT ANYONE'S ANYTHING

NOT ANYONE'S ANYTHING

IAN WILLIAMS

Freehand Books gratefully acknowledges the support of the Canada Council for the Arts for its publishing program. ¶ Freehand Books, an imprint of Broadview Press Inc., gratefully acknowledges the financial support for its publishing program provided by the Government of Canada through the Canada Book Fund.

Canada Council   Conseil des Arts
for the Arts   du Canada

Freehand Books
412 – 815 1st Street SW Calgary, Alberta T2P 1N3
www.freehand-books.com

Book orders: Broadview Press Inc.
280 Perry Street, Unit 5 Peterborough, Ontario K9J 2J4
Telephone: 705-743-8990 Fax: 705-743-8353
customerservice@broadviewpress.com
www.broadviewpress.com

/ LIBRARY AND ARCHIVES CANADA CATALOGUING IN PUBLICATION /
Williams, Ian, 1979–
Not anyone's anything / Ian William.

ISBN 978-1-55111-995-3

        1. Title.

PS8645.I4448N68 2011   C813'.6   C2011-900547-6

Edited by Robyn Read
Book design by Natalie Olsen, Kisscut Design
Author photo by Luke Khomeriki

Printed on FSC recycled paper and bound in Canada

FOR MY MOTHER.
FOR EVERYTHING.

o o o

I

II

TRIOS

shall be sentenced to imprisonment for life
is liable to imprisonment for a term not exceeding ten years
is liable to imprisonment for a term not exceeding seven years

60% of black children grow up without a father
43% of first marriages end in divorce or separation within fifteen years
Divorce rates are highest during the fourth year of marriage

While
Then
Next

III

I

000

NOT ANYONE'S ANYTHING

We try to break up every night before he goes home. It sounds so high school, doesn't it? *Break up. Me and Goran broke up. Girl, you won't believe who broke up.* Then comes the R&B heartbreak anthems, one hand up in the air testifying. Then comes the girls' night out, girl power, *we don't need no man, Ima survivah, yeah!* This is exactly why Goran and I have to break up before the night's through, to ward off all that drama. I don't have time for that.

"Me? Is it me?" Goran asks. We're walking from class to his dorm on the west side of University of Toronto, then I'll walk the rest of the way to Koreatown alone. "You're dropping the course because of me. There's no other reason far as I can tell."

"You got me. I plan my life around you," I say.

"No shame in that, babe."

Babe registers, but I ignore it. "I don't have room for Korean."

"But you're Korean."

I let that one go too. "With the store and the other summer course, I'm just maxed out."

"And I'm dicking around in grad school."

"Pretty much." From what he tells me, it just sounds like he's reading comic books. *They're graphic novels,* he says in my head. Whatever. Try Applied Econometrics then talk to me.

"Was the vocab quiz that bad for you?" he asks.

I hand him the rolled-up quiz and wait for him to gloat.

"Sixteen. Ouch." He slurps in his breath.

"All right, Einstein. Take it easy."

"Didn't you study, Soo? I got eighteen and I'm not even — "

I wag my jaw. We've reached his dorm. Goran cups my elbow and gives me a greasy, gold-chain, chest-hair smile.

"You can't drop, Soo-bella" he says. "How you gonna throw away our one week together as if it's nothing to you?"

I start walking. He runs ahead and intercepts me.

"Seriously, Soo, Soo Soo Soo, sixteen isn't bad. Just make yourself some flash cards and go through them every night."

There's a brief, stunned silence before I let him have it: "My cumulative GPA is 3.86, so I think I know a little bit about study-ing. You know, with my Korean smart-genes and all. I might not be in quote unquote grad school yet, but I can figure out how to memorize some words."

"Take it or leave it." His eyes are grey. He looks geometric. A sundial for a nose, the rest of his triangular face divided into planes — planes of his cheeks, planes of his jaw, planes of his eyelids. A man based on a Picasso. His hair looks like a helmet made from a spiky animal.

I smile tightly. "Ciao. It's been good knowing you."

This is breakup number one, where I don't hurt Goran as much as I intend to, because, I guess, well, technically, we're not going out.

I know what he's thinking as I walk away. She's such a typical Asian girl, all she cares about are her grades, and pleasing her par-ents, and when any little thing goes wrong in a course she's quick to drop it. As if it's a crime to care. And I'm not typical. You're typical, you smug, condescending *kojaengi*. Try to tell me how to study. 3.86 yo. After work, I'm so dropping him. It. I mean *it*. Korean. Do you? I do. *Do you?* Please. Like he's anything. Are you mad because he beat you on the quiz or because he doesn't have the hots for you? I don't have time anyway. Because you spend all your time working at the convenience store or because you're studying for quizzes you can't ace? Listen, I've got my priorities straight.

Sixteen isn't bad. Like hell it's not. I registered for Intermediate Korean to offset the Econometrics grade this summer. Twelve weeks, M W 5:00-7:30 p.m. On the advice of some Korean friends, I faked my level of fluency to get in. *Tell Professor Yoon that your parents mostly speak English to you at home, that you speak a little Korean to your grandparents or something, but that you can't read well or understand too much.* Not much of lie. When I was a kid, my parents sent me to Korean school on Saturday mornings, then that fizzled out, which means I read like a second grader. My parents have a mix of embarrassment and pride about my ability. In Korea, it would pretty much amount to illiteracy. *She's really Canadian*, they tell our long-distance relatives. *She can't even read Korean.* I understand enough Korean to understand that.

As I'm walking to the store, the R&B backup singers begin in my head. *Tell me how you go'n drop him, Soo? It. Will you drop it like Newton's apple? or like a bad stock? like it's hot?*

(I'll miss the big social experiment that is — was, it's dead to me — Intermediate Korean. It was made up of sixteen other Korean girls of varying Koreanness, from cover-your-mouth-when-laughing girls to girls like me, born in Canada, Korean more by ethnicity than culture, like non-religious Jews. Most of the class fell in the middle — here since age ten or eleven, a hint of a Korean accent when pronouncing unfamiliar English words.)

*like leaves in the fall? like rain in the spring? like a man crossin'
the Falls on a tightrope in the wind?*

(And I'll miss Goran, the one white guy in the class, the lone
ranger. There. I admit it. First class he sat his gangly self next to
me and said, *Is this Baroque Art?* I said, *Korean*. He said, *Ooh
honeychile, I in the wrong place*. But he's actually a PhD student
in East Asian Studies, trying to fulfill a third language requirement.
He's "researching" Japanese graphic novels although he's Serbian
— his parents — and accepts his destiny of becoming Toronto's most
overqualified burger flipper when he graduates. A side effect of
the comics is that he thinks he can be anybody: Korean, Serbian,
Newfie, Japanese, Jamaican, Italian, Quebecois, Ghetto. A week in
his company and I've already adopted *ciao* and *yo*.)

*like piano? like ballet? like a bird gettin' shot? like the Times
Square ball when you count down the clock?*

(Goran's Korean is okay for a non-Korean. Cute. Like a Shih
Tzu trying to bark with the big dogs. By unspoken agreement,
the girls in the class have adopted him as a younger brother, our
dongseng, whispering pronunciation to him or tapping a spot in
our books when he's called on. I won't lie, more than once when
I tuned out of lecture it was because I was thinking of presenting
him to my parents. *Say something in Korean. Go on*.)

*like a plane outta gas? like a bomb on Japan? Girl, after work,
you go'n drop it like a man?*

But everyone who comes into the convenience store that
evening is so pleasant. Keep the change. Out of calling cards?
No problem. Even my father, calling from the North York store,
says I should eat some ice cream bars (while I study, granted).
Making small talk, an old woman asks what I am taking at

university. I tell her Commerce, with an emphasis in Management. She says she used to teach Korean at Ulsan National University. I tell her I am trying to improve my Korean. And the old woman says—she is like a hundred and forty, *old* old; only an old woman could say what she says—칠 전 팔 기. Then she translates in her careful English: *Seven time fall, eight time rise. Even I try learn English.*

o o o

When I walk into Korean two evenings later, I expect some noticeable change, the way you expect the world to sympathize with you when you're freshly heartbroken. The class is still in the basement of University College, full of girls cooing and showing each other videos on their cell phones. The windows still start at our necks and are filled halfway with brown leaves from last fall.

Goran is asking the girl who sits on his other side about her quiz grade. Perfect. She's trying to be humble with her one double eyelid.

"It was so easy," she says.

I fan myself. This is the day some zealous campus organization —the kind trying to do important things by being as trivial as possible—has fought for, the day when the whole university shuts down air conditioning to save energy.

"Hot enough for ya?" Goran says when he sees me. He's Texan today.

"I'm going to round up those kids and taser them."

One-eyelid says, "We're just trying to show that we care about the planet."

Oh shut up. "I didn't mean you, Sophie. It's the others who take it too far."

She drops her voice. "Goran said you were dropping the course because you failed the quiz."

"Now you wait a minute, partner. I didn't say *fail.*"

"You really bombed it, Soo? *Jeongmal?*"

Professor Yoon is waiting for our attention. I pull out a stack of flash cards and place them on the corner of my desk. Bring it, sister.

o o o

Three weeks into the course, Goran and I get locked in this great desultory conversation that makes him extend his walk beyond his dorm, past Honest Ed's, right into the Korean district. Koreatown is twenty years behind Korea, my cousins said when they visited. Compact, lacking in luxury, it's as if the people who immigrated and set up these businesses are stuck in a time warp. There's been some buzz about gentrification, but the higher-end businesses can't take root among the movie rental places, diner-style restaurants, and fruit stands.

Goran is fascinated. His head swivels around. In an accent that's meant to sound Asian, he says, *exotic.* It comes out, *erotic.*

"Like Vegas," he says. "Like Disneyworld. Like a Korean Chinatown."

As he's saying this, a man dressed like my father with his pants belted high on his stomach hawks up phlegm and spits it on the street. Goran stares after it like he wants a sample.

My parents' convenience store is on a side street off Bloor. This one isn't too impressive. The one in North York, where my parents spend most of their time, is newer, bigger, and brings in more business. Goran reads the sign, 코너 김, "Kohnuh Kim," Corner Kim. I live in the flat above the store. It's walking distance to campus, a couple of subway stops at the most, plus it saves my parents having to pay room and board for me. When I graduate, they plan to lease the upstairs flat to a couple who wants to open an upscale coffeehouse. They're starting to think of themselves as entrepreneurs and not lowly convenience store owners. It's a class complex. Don't even say *dry cleaner* around them.

"You've got chimes and everything," Goran says when we step inside.

"We got your Twinkies, we got your magazines, we got your lotto tickets, your canned food, your frozen treats, your milk, your pop, your toiletries, your stationary." It's all visible from where we're standing. I point up to a corner of the room where a surveillance camera is mounted to the ceiling. "We even got your reality show."

The guy at the counter looks up from texting and smiles deliciously.

We got your spy too.

His real name is Dae-ho, but he calls himself Prince Ho. He's a Korean student who has finished an Intensive English course, doesn't want to go back to Korea just yet, and has convinced my parents to hire him illegally. For less than minimum wage, he seems content to work the store around my schedule, spending his days reading the sports papers and practicing his English on the underaged teenagers who try to buy cigarettes.

"What's shaking?" Prince Ho says. He likes to try out phrases from a pocket English guide, which must have been written in the nineties by a posse of men with afro picks in their hair.

"I am pleased to make your acquaintance," Goran says stiffly in Korean.

"You are — no, wait — you *must be* in Soo's Korean language class. Your Korean ability is the bomb."

In Korean, "Thank you. You also have learned English too very well."

I intervene. I dip into the freezer, put an ice cream sandwich on the counter for Prince Ho. That's for his silence. I grab a couple more and lure Goran outside.

"Ain't nothing but a chicken wing," Prince Ho shouts as we're leaving.

All it takes for Goran to forget about his truncated conversation with Prince Ho is a bite into the ice cream sandwich, which he does by wrapping his lips over his teeth and closing down. I have a brief moment where I wonder whether I burned enough calories walking here to pre-metabolize 450 calories. We are sitting on the front steps, blocking the entrance to the store, while Goran reads the signs around him, then pulls out flash cards from his bag. His printing, both in Korean and English, is so neat that it looks like he's been tracing computer fonts.

"Quiz me," he says.

The sandwiches, the flash cards, our pronunciation, our concentration — it's all very sloppy.

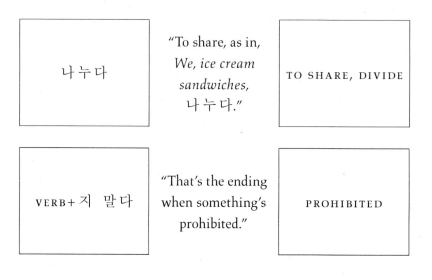

나누다	"To share, as in, *We, ice cream sandwiches,* 나누다."	TO SHARE, DIVIDE
VERB+지 말다	"That's the ending when something's prohibited."	PROHIBITED

울다	"To cry, as in, *Soo cries like a little baby whenever Goran leaves.*"	TO CRY

Even after we finish the sandwiches, he keeps asking for one more word. Last one. One more. It's twenty minutes before we split up and Goran goes tra-la-la-ing down the street.

o o o

About 11:30 one Wednesday night at the store, while I'm calculating the lowest grades I could get in Econometrics and Korean and still keep my 3.86, the chimes go off and in comes Goran's geometric head. It's the first time he's found his way here on his own. He's looking up at the chimes, shaking his head as if to say, *Got me again, you darn buggers.*

"I'm out of soap," he says. "I've been showering with dishwashing liquid."

"I did not need to know that."

"I can take my business elsewhere, you know."

"Soap's in aisle four," I say. "Next to toothpaste and mouthwash."

Goran's head floats above the shelves, then it disappears for a few seconds, then it resurfaces. He walks to the counter, package of soap under his arm, counting out change in his palm and complaining about our prices.

As I'm ringing up the soap, he says, "Aren't you supposed to ask if I found everything I needed today?"

"People usually know what they want when they come in."

"Ask me."

"Did you find everything you needed today? Can I interest you in any of our impulse items?" I brandish my hand over the gum display.

"No, man. Me nah satisfy." Jamaican. "Me lookin' for some flash card dem."

"They're upstairs. You want to study now?"

"Me say me wah play. What so hard in dat to understan'? Me go watch de store while you go check de back."

I install him behind the counter and head upstairs to get the cards. I can tell that I've just fulfilled one of his fantasies, like seeing a cockpit or riding up front in a police cruiser.

"Let's make things interesting." I say, coming down the stairs. "If you can do thirty-five flash cards in a minute, I'll give you the soap for free."

Goran eyes the surveillance camera.

"We won't go out of business over soap," I reassure him. "I'll just mess up someone's change later."

He pretends to look horrified. I outline the rules quickly. I'll hold up the cards one at a time, Korean side facing Goran, English facing me, and he'll have a minute to translate a stack of thirty-five. He can pass on two cards. Then we'll switch. If he gets through his cards without a screw-up, he wins. If I get through mine, I win.

It takes Goran nine rounds to win the soap for keeps. It's enough for him to develop a gambling addiction. Around round five, he would have had the soap but risked it for a bag of malt balls, those with the nasty aftertaste, and lost both. And now, a few rounds later, he wins back the soap, the malt balls, and a pack of cheese curls. I form a snowplow with my hands and push the winnings toward him. Because he has nothing to bet, when it's my turn, he offers up his body for punishment.

"If you win, you get to stomp on my foot."

"Can I jump?"

"If you win, you get to punch me as hard as you can."

"Can I knee you in the groin?"

"If you win, you get to give me a purple nurple."

"Are you getting off on this?"

I win all of those. By now, it's after one in the morning. I flick off the neon *OPEN* sign. I have some work to do for my other course before I can go to sleep, meaning it's time for Goran to go.

"One more game," Goran says. His eyes are so finely outlined by his lashes they seem hand-drawn. "One more and I'll leave you alone."

"Stakes?"

"Championship prize," he says. British. "I win, and you, young lady, will have the pleasure of dating one of Toronto's finest bachelors."

I look around, searching.

"You win," he continues, "and I suppose I shall have to endure the disgrace of my family and date a convenience store mogul."

"Lucky me."

"Do we have a deal?"

Not quite. "If you win, fine, I'll—whatever. But if I win, it's over. We break up. Tonight."

"The lady's offer is most perplexing."

We both win.

o o o

Haven't you been hoping that Goran would take your hand between both of his and press it to his lips like a repressed hero in a movie? I am paying attention to Professor Yoon. I am. I am. Don't you want to kiss Goran's sundial nose with your own the way Eskimos do so their lips don't stick together, a tongue on a flagpole? 마음 means *heart*. I missed 마음씨. Damn. If you cut off Goran's head and dumped it in the forest, wouldn't it look like a porcupine or a large hedgehog? Let's see, 씨 means *mister*. Was he ever Pinhead for Halloween? Professor Yoon's talking like her words have an expiration date. Does he have spiky hair down there like a brush? He doesn't have anything down there. Can Goran tell the difference between your own eyelashes and the ones you're wearing? I don't know what you're talking about. Why don't you touch his thigh right now, bat your eyes, and ask him for the meaning of 마음씨? And you can shut the 마음씨 up. Why did you come back to Korean after freestyling about dropping it? The old, old woman said she was learning English. How old was she? Two hundred plus. Like men in the Old Testament. Did their wives live as long and have children into their hundreds? Women usually outlive men. Will all the girls in this class outlive Goran and have his babies into their forties? This is not a polygamous cult. And that's sick. (A) How many of the sixteen girls in this class are menstrual right now and (B) do you think Goran can sense it? I can't even sense it. What about (A)? Two, three maybe. How many eggs do you have left? Plenty. What percentage of them are duds, babies with thick calves and moon faces? My calves are right for my body type. For my body type, my calves are right. Is your self-esteem any higher for repeating that? My calves are right. Does Goran go to Sophie's dorm room on the off nights with his flash cards, his sundial nose, geometric face, and spiky hair? It's a free country. Do you believe that or are you just playing tough? It would be a betrayal. Is he bragging to his friends that he's banging two Asian sluts at the same time? No one's getting banged. At all or at the same time? I am not. Why didn't you object to the word *slut*? My objection was implied. Would he choose Sophie over you because she is an environmental activist, which at least shows that she cares about her unborn children's future? She's flat. But she is thinner than you, right? My body is mine and I will honour it. Doesn't she look better in skirts like that topaz number she's wearing because she doesn't have fat man-calves? Her clothes are probably made from recycled paper. Do you look like a butch compared to Sophie even with your fake eyelashes? Pass. Since Sophie beat you on the first quiz, does that mean she's naturally smarter and has a higher GPA than you? She's flat. If Goran ends up with Sophie, would you make up stories about you and Prince Ho to get him jealous, let him see what he's missing? That would be pathetic. Do you consider Goran a hunka hunka burning love? Mmhmm. Do you, Soo-ha Kim, take this man, Goran Danilovic, to be your lawfully wedded husband, to have and to hold, in sickness and health, for richer or poorer, for as long as you both shall live? I do. Did you find everything you needed today? I did. Why did you add the bit about breaking up at the end of Wednesday's game? The lady is herself perplexed. Would he have kissed you by now? Baby. Does his mouth taste like mouthwash, like gum, like sleep, or like milk? Like words. Which ones? Korean.

000

In trying to understand why I insist on breaking up during the last rounds of flash cards on the nights Goran comes by, my voice and I have duked it out and reached these conclusions: (A) I don't have time for a relationship, with the store and the summer courses and all, (B) I don't want Goran to think that I want to get physically involved with him, (C) I can't afford to have Goran go ga ga over me in public and compromise my integrity as a serious student, (D) I don't want to turn into one of those girls who totes around bags from high-end stores and complains when her man doesn't call her every night. What else? (E) my highfalutin reason: he turns almost everything into a big joke and hides behind various identities to mask his own, potentially unformed, identity. For all the above reasons, when Goran leaves the store at night, I file him, I try to file him, in a folder called *Distraction* and close the drawer. Except the next time I see him, I can't help but run my fingers over the tops of manila folders — *Store Responsibilities, Issues With Parents, Issues with Body, GPA, Korean Course, Distraction* — and retrieve his dossier.

One night at the store, as we're playing with a new set of flash cards, another distraction walks in on us. Prince Ho. He claims he needs a lighter. When he sees Goran behind the counter, the electricity in his face flicks on. It's a two-for-one special: he's thinking, *opportunity to practice English with a native speaker* and *blackmail Soo for having a man around at this hour.* Goran lights up too. A real Korean. He and Prince Ho try sentences out on each other, like they're playing Battleship. Goran in Korean, Prince Ho in — I don't even want to claim it — American.

Goran: "On this beautiful night, my friend, Soo, and I are studying."

Prince Ho: "You are a dirty dog, homie. Is Soo all that and a bag of chips?"

Me: "I'm right here. Don't talk about me as if I'm not here."

Prince Ho [to me]: "Talk to the hand, 'cause the face ain't listening."

Me, holding up a lighter: "Free if you leave now."

He grabs the lighter from my hand, like it's a limited time offer, and goes out to smoke. We can see him through a non-postered square of glass, drawing in deeply and blowing out.

"Let's call it a night," I say. Reason C has already been transgressed.

"Patience, young one." Aboriginal. "We still have championship round between your tribe and mine."

"Make it quick." We've actually been playing the last round for twenty minutes now.

"For the union between tribe Kim and tribe Danilovic."

"Or the breakup thereof."

Prince Ho is petting a dog and talking to its owner outside. Poor woman. Goran wins his game in superb form, whizzing through the cards, passing on only one. He pumps his fists, looks at me first as if I were an opponent that got dunked on, then as if I were a conquest he recently clobbered and dragged back to his cave by the hair.

Prince Ho stands up outside and jiggles the leash.

"Quick," I say.

Goran starts my game. I'm doing fine until I look out and see Prince Ho flick away his cigarette. His mouth continues to make strange, overly dramatic English shapes. Focus, Soo. He'll be inside soon. Is he getting her number? No way. What does 욕 (하 다) mean?

"Time!" Goran shouts. "You lose, babe!"

The chimes. Prince Ho. "She lose what?"

Goran actually hops over the counter, takes Prince Ho by the neck and tousles his hair, a locker room gesture. In Korean, Goran says, "I will tell you on the way to my home at the university."

"You better not," I say.

"Party! Party!" Prince Ho says.

Goran: "Alcohol please."

"Woo!"

"Goran, I was distracted."

Together: "Woo!"

"It doesn't count."

"It counts!"

Goran blows me a kiss. Prince Ho blows me a kiss. Chimes.

I turn over the losing card.

```
┌─────────────────────┐        ┌─────────────────────┐
│                     │        │                     │
│    욕 (하 다)         │        │    (TO) CURSE,      │
│                     │        │  SLANDER, DESIRE    │
│                     │        │                     │
└─────────────────────┘        └─────────────────────┘
```

o o o

That was a Monday. In class on Wednesday, Goran puts his arm around the back of my chair all macho, all I-own-this-stuff-right-here. The sixteen other girls are tittering. I know it. They're writing notes in the margins of their books then scratching them out. Sophie flashes me a triumphant, *So you're into white guys, eh?*

Immediately after class I have to break up with Goran, even if it means I'll owe Prince Ho overtime. I take Goran into the Robarts library cafeteria, and break out the cards. He can't understand why his woman is so businesslike.

"Don't call me that."

"Call you what? My woman?" he says. I don't know who he's trying to be. A pimp maybe.

"I'm not anyone's anything."

"Correction. You mine," he says. Then he goes back to being some version of himself. "You want an iced coffee?"

"No." See reason D. "Sit down and let's play."

"My roommates want to meet you."

The plural registers. "You've been broadcasting this?"

"I wouldn't call it *broadcasting*. I was telling them about the last game. How about you, me, the fellas, maybe Prince Ho meet up at — "

"I have to work."

"Every day, twenty-four hours?"

Here's where I lose it because I hear the accusation coming—all you do is work and study. It's my impulse when I'm cornered to wave around a broken bottle and fight dirty.

"If you can find time in my schedule," I say, "to hang around drinking beer and reading comic books with you and your roommates, then fine I'll meet them. I'll just stick a dummy up at the register, put on my fishnets, and you can show off your Asian ho to all your boys."

"Works for me."

"You know what? I don't even want to play. We're not going out," I declare. I gather the cards and get ready to go.

"That's just like you." He remains infuriatingly cool. He makes circles with his palms. "In control of everything."

"Don't act like you know me."

"If you want out, you have to play for it. So *you* sit down, try controlling yourself instead of everything else, and relax." Goran takes out his wallet. "Now, I'm going for an iced coffee. You want one?"

I shake my head. Who is this man, talking to you like you talk to him? I don't know. Do you want to knee him in the groin? Real hard this time.

When Goran comes back, he says he needs to warm up. His warm-ups are as long as his 'final' rounds. Then our bets turn into dares. That afternoon I have to get a guy's number. He gets a girl's number. I shoplift a muffin, get caught, say *I forgot to pay*, end up borrowing money to pay for it. Goran swears at a work-study student at the checkout. I walk into the guy's bathroom and stay there for thirty seconds.

Finally I tell him I have to get to the store so we need to play the championship round right away. No more *patience, young one.*

The vocabulary is the same as Monday's, but Goran falters on words he should know. He loses his game. This is it. For the breakup. The white-rabbit feeling — *I don't have time* — seizes me.

Sixty seconds later, I point my two forefingers in Goran's face and say, "Dumped."

He scrapes his chair back, tosses the flash cards on the table, and leaves. Dumped.

o o o

Do you know what you did to drive away the only guy who's shown you attention since you've been at university? I'm working right now. Working at what, spinsterhood? At meeting the needs of this valued customer looking for cooking oil. Who's meeting your needs? I don't have any needs. Are you bionic? I don't need no man who only wants to affect accents and play games. Why don't you hook up with a producer and turn that into an R&B track? We don't carry extra virgin olive oil. Are you sure about that, pumpkin? Cruel. Is now the time to use Prince Ho to make Goran jealous? Goran is utterly uninterested in me. Why can't you understand that? Why can't you? Would you take a 0.1 drop in your GPA to replay that moment in Robarts three weeks ago? 0.06 max. Why did you overreact? See reasons A through E. Is it possibly because Professor Yoon and Sophie saw Goran put his arm around your chair? Sophie should be tied up in a burlap sack and drowned. Why so *rarrrw*? He was thumbing her number into his phone. Do you think they're studying or sleeping together on her ergonomic mattress? He never asked me for my number. Who is watching you from behind the surveillance camera, your mother, your father, or God? He never asked me. Do you have anything resembling a plan? I'll apologize soon as we're alone. Shouldn't you lose a little weight first? I will not buy into unrealistic standards of beauty. Are you lonely? Pass. Who are your friends? Pass. How do you feel when you open the store in the morning and you're greeted by rows of dog food, kitty litter, stationary, soap, toothpaste, nuts, cigarettes, the chimes, the register, gum?

o o o

Prince Ho says I need to drink some soju with him and his friends. My mother, when I see her, takes the ends of my hair in her hands and says split ends are a sign of insufficient protein. My father wants to know about my quiz grades in Korean. My mother says neurotransmitters also need protein to function optimally. Prince Ho says I need to get drunk. A customer wants to know why we don't sell soap for sensitive skin. My mother says, Protein. My father says, Korean. No old lady comes back with the right word.

o o o

Although Goran doesn't come by the store anymore, we still see each other in class, but he's doing this avoidance thing where he shows up a minute before Professor Yoon, then on the break he goes to the washroom and loiters in the hallway reading bulletin boards, then he comes back in and talks to Sophie about hybrid cars or recycling programs in eastern Europe, then after class he stands in line with all the other kiss-ups, notebook in hand, waiting to ask Yoon something. He's civil enough to me, not warm like he used to be. When he can't talk to Sophie, he asks me how Econometrics is going. A few weeks of his civility and I'm like screw it, you know. If he doesn't want to talk to me, fine. My life is full enough.

Then, on an acid-hot night in early August, a week before finals, minutes before closing, the chimes jangle — the return of Goran's geometric head and sundial nose. Although I'm looking at his face, it's as if I'm looking at myself from his point of view. No makeup, hair in a ponytail and poked through the back of a baseball cap, oversized T-shirt, reading with my cheeks on my knuckles. I've regressed.

He greets me in Korean with a little nod. I sit up straight. One of us needs to say something witty quick. Or should I apologize now? I have one prepared: Goran, I'm not sure what went wrong with our friendship. All I know is that your attitude toward me has changed. [Pause, 2, 3.] All right, I know what went wrong [the false start is part of the apology]. I'm sorry for going ballistic on you that day in Robarts. It was just that you put your arm around my chair, and you got this macho attitude that I really hate. It's like how my dad acts with my mom when he's trying to impress people, like she's a chess piece [an exaggeration, but I'm playing the stereotype of Asian gender roles to win me sympathy points]. Anyhow, I'm sorry. I don't blame you. I was rude and you didn't deserve that.

He approaches the counter. Maybe he will take my face in both his hands and kiss me like a milkshake.

"Goran," I say. "I'm not sure what [He's frowning. Why's he frowning?] went wrong with our friendship. All I know is that your"

"Nothing wrong. How you say, I want play flash card with girl who live here."

Easy as that. And yet, because I spent so long constructing that apology, I feel cheated out of saying it. What about my simile, *like she's a chess piece*? Start again.

"Goran, I'm not sure — "

"Girl with flash card not here?" he asks, louder.

"She's here," I say. "She's here."

He doesn't seem himself.

It's closing time. We won't be interrupted. I shut down the store while Goran goes up and down the aisles with a basket, pulling items from the shelves for prizes.

"Chocolate-covered peanuts, almonds, or cashews?" he asks.

"All the above."

"Barbecue chips or all dressed?"

"All dressed."

I take the tray out of the cash register. I should be more discreet when transporting cash. But look at him, he's not interested in where I take the money. He looks off. A little dark around the eyes. Did Sophie spurn him? Don't say her name again. Is it safe to lock yourself inside the store with a man so spiky-headed?

There are hundreds of cards under the counter. I started storing them there in July. Just in case. Goran brings the basket of prize food behind the counter and sits on the floor cross-legged. He yanks my wrist to pull me down to the floor and announces the stakes. "First round is for the entire basket. If I win, the food's mine."

"What's *win* this time?" I say.

"Thirty-five cards. Thirty seconds. Three passes, max."

"You mean sixty seconds."

"No, I mean thirty seconds." He makes two fists and cracks his knuckles. "What, you can't hang?"

During the first game, Goran is in a furor, and it looks like he'll get through the cards, but he runs out of time with five left. He clobbers his forehead with the heel of his hand. He's hungry. I could just give him the food. I owe him that much. Or I could start losing on purpose if I were the type to throw games away. I don't mean to, but I lose my game anyway.

We play another round for the food and he loses. He drums his thighs. He says, "Forget the food."

There's a fine layer of wet on him. Reminds me of kiwi fuzz. Moisture in the dimple over his lip. And he's more tanned than he was even last week.

"Forget the food," he says again. "New prize."

I see where this is going. "Me?"

"You got weird last time."

"I won't get weird."

"Right."

"Try me."

Goran jumps up and steps over me. I have to duck to escape getting hit by his crotch. I assume he's going to check the shelves for some non-food prize item. Soap.

"When you came in tonight," I shout, "were you supposed to sound Korean?"

"I was going for Chinese."

"Racist bastard."

"What?"

"I called you a racist bastard." It's easier to talk to him when he's not visible. The confessional effect. I should try the apology again, pick up at *I'm sorry for going ballistic on you that day in Robarts. It was just that you put your arm around my chair, and you got this macho attitude that I really*

The lights go off. Goran steps back over my shoulder and sits down facing me.

"What's going on?"

"New game," he says. "Strip flash cards."

I hesitate. "I don't know, Goran. Playing for skin, that's so — "

"Sleazy, high school, drunken, unlike what either of us would do, all the above."

All the above? He's being me.

He's already shuffling the cards. "Look, it's dark. I can't even see you."

But I think there is enough light filtering in from the outside to see each other — if he can read the cards in this light, then sure as hell he can read a nipple. As the one recently forgiven, I know I should be accommodating. There's a challenge implicit in this game. I can either be a bookish Asian girl or a hot, liberated spring break chick who will be a good sport and flash a carload of men when she loses a bet, after protesting just enough not to seem like a slut. Have I protested enough?

"Are you sure you can't see me?" I say.

He feels around as if blind.

I suck in my breath. "I don't know, Goran."

"Do the math," he says. The tone. He's still being me. "Compare what you're wearing to what I'm wearing."

By that count, I have him beat. He's wearing shiny, synthetic soccer shorts to his knees, a white undershirt, and sneakers, no socks, *probably* underwear. That's four or five items, depending on whether sneakers constitute one item or two. I have a baseball cap, T-shirt, pants, shoes, socks, bra, panties, elastic in my hair, clips. If desperate, I could also count the studs in my ears. Puts me at a two to one advantage.

He hands me a stack of cards. Decision's made.

First round, Goran loses a shoe. My turn — it's the pressure — I have to give up my baseball cap.

"Not just the hat, all hair accessories," Goran says.

So I remove the elastic.

"And the clips."

"Then you have to remove the other shoe. Since we're counting families of clothing."

Next round, we're both safe. Then I lose my shoes, then my socks.

Flash. Prince Ho entering arm in arm with Sophie. He says, *What's the dealio? Together are you getting jiggy?* And slyly, *Your dad know about your new daddy?* Sophie's laugh is from a class above me, organic, full of wind power, emission-free. Her legs look fantastic. Her breasts too, like a woman from the future in a comic book. Her GPA is printed on her shirt. 3.92. Prince Ho says something to her in Korean that I can't understand and he laughs until he snorts and she laughs her emission-free laugh and Goran laughs a Korean laugh.

Two rounds after that, Goran loses his shirt. He flexes, crosses his wrists so his arms look like two parentheses. His straining trapezius muscles seem the most natural continuation of his triangular face.

"This is the big deal?" I say.

"We haven't hit the big deal yet, babe."

"Shut up and deal."

Flash. My father entering the store. The vision has the quality of a surveillance camera recording. His shirt is tucked in, pants high, hair parted and dyed too black, skin a deep grey colour that would translate as orange. There's a moment of terror, when Goran and I freeze under the counter. On seeing us, my father has a second or two to decide whether he should kill Goran, then cook up a story about robbery, rape, self-defence. And why mutilate the body, Mr. Kim? Temporary insanity. He is old school when it comes to torture —poverty, military service, growing up with stories of the Japanese.

We need to stop this. Cut the game short. My father's messing up my concentration, telepathically screwing me up from North York. Or it's the danger I see in Goran's scrawny chest, the T of dark hair running from over his nipples down through his stomach into the elastic of his shorts.

He's an outie.

I'm willing to declare his shirtlessness victory. The decision of what to give up next is making me hotter. It's between exposing my thick calves or my soft stomach. I'm an innie.

"I'm satisfied," I say after a few safe rounds.

"But we're not done." With two fingers, he tucks my sock into the mouth of one of his sneakers. The gesture's obscene. Or maybe it's not. Strip flash cards turns everything kinky.

"I'm getting tired," I say instead of *I don't want to play anymore.*

"Last round," he says. "Then I'll go home."

"Last round," I repeat.

"Last round."

We tighten up the rules. In thirty seconds, no wrong answers, no passes.

Flash. My mother entering after my father. She is wearing a mauve velour suit I bought for her last Christmas, a visor, low heels—she has an odd way of dressing things up. She does not even look at Goran, just zeroes in on me, reading my hair, my unpainted toenails, making bizarre connections: *this is why you don't play piano! You get pregnant in two years because of* kojaengi, *end of school, end of career, just stay home and cook* bop.

귀찮다. Goran loses his game on that word, means *irritating*, means he loses his shorts. He stands up and takes them off by turning around and bending over straight-legged so he's mooning me. His briefs are black, as I somehow knew they would be. The hairs on his calves, on his thighs, are black and long like his chest hair.

진찰 (하다) did it for me. Between my pants and my T-shirt, I choose to surrender my shirt. Goran keeps his face still. The voice, the voice. Do you think he's enjoying? Why is he so? How fat do I? Should I try laxa? We need to stop.

I cross my arms and hold my shoulders. I look at the pile to
the side of us where we've been throwing our clothes. They rub
together more intimately than we ever have. I look at Goran in his
underwear, his sundial nose, his moustache of sweat, the T of hair
on his chest, the curve of muscle where one calf sits on his heel,
and from the base of my spine begins an agony like a fist opening
and closing.

Flash. Us. Goran kneels and leans forward. I'll say he made the
choice one-sided. I wanted to. I didn't want to. I was taken up, was
Scarlett O'Haraed. He stretches his languid body over mine on
the floor of the convenience store, our heads under the register,
my hand at the back of his neck, where his magnificent geometry
begins, the other gripping his tricep. He says one Korean word
over and over, turning it over in his foreign mouth, 사랑, *sarang*,
사랑해요 *sarang heyo*, 사랑스럽다 *sarangseureopda*, *sarang*,
사랑, *sarang*.

"Now we're done," I say.

"You're so close to humiliating me. One loss away."

"I've humiliated you already."

"Last time," he says. "One more."

"You always say *one more* and we go on for half an hour."

"I'll put everything on this round. What do you want?"

"You have to go home," I say. The occasion calls for something
worse, like his going in women's clothing. "You have to go home
and you can never come back here. Goran, I'm serious. I win this
round and we're done for good."

"Let's do it."

"Or you want to cut your losses now?"

"Oh, I'll play. But if I win, we go out for real."

"Fine."

"Out places," Goran adds. "Like real people."

"Fine."

"We sleep together."

"Wait, wait."

"We boogie."

"What do you take me for?"

"Soo, fourteen-year-old kids are getting it on." He adjusts himself before he continues. "In language you can understand — how can I say this? The maturity date of your stock has come. How else? The expiration date of your wares is here."

I can't tell if he's joking or who he's being. Is it me still?

I laugh because I don't know what else to do. Goran simply waits for me to finish, unsmiling.

"That's a yes," he says for me.

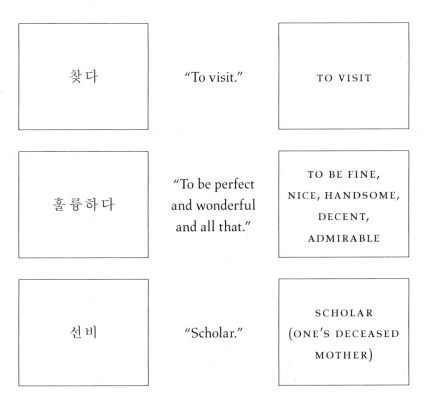

찾 다	"To visit."	TO VISIT
훌 륭 하 다	"To be perfect and wonderful and all that."	TO BE FINE, NICE, HANDSOME, DECENT, ADMIRABLE
선 비	"Scholar."	SCHOLAR (ONE'S DECEASED MOTHER)

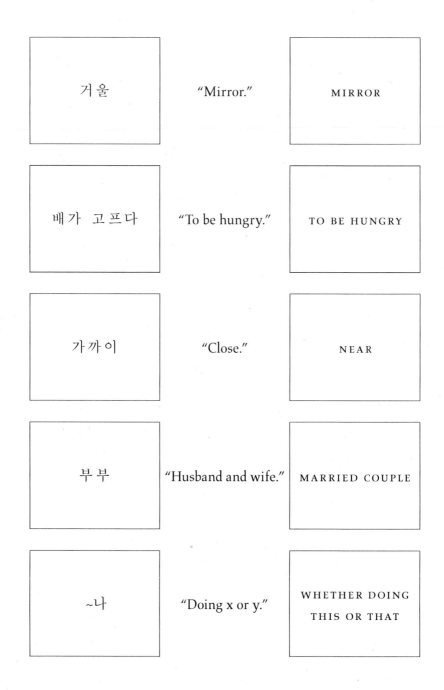

거울	"Mirror."	MIRROR
배가 고프다	"To be hungry."	TO BE HUNGRY
가까이	"Close."	NEAR
부부	"Husband and wife."	MARRIED COUPLE
~나	"Doing x or y."	WHETHER DOING THIS OR THAT

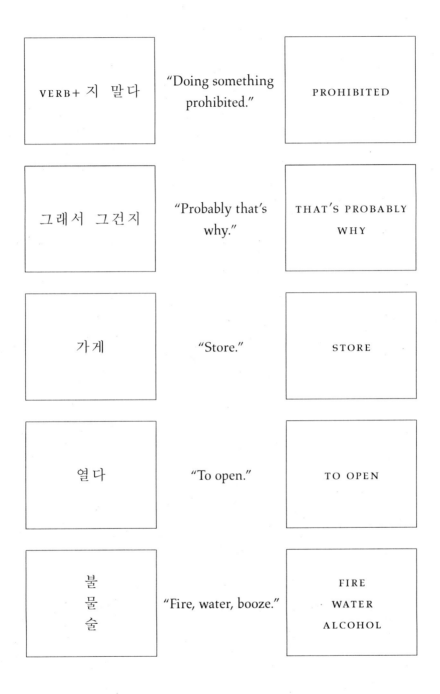

VERB+ 지 말다	"Doing something prohibited."	PROHIBITED
그래서 그건지	"Probably that's why."	THAT'S PROBABLY WHY
가게	"Store."	STORE
열다	"To open."	TO OPEN
불 물 술	"Fire, water, booze."	FIRE WATER ALCOHOL

목소리	"Voice."	VOICE
싫어하다	"To hate."	TO DISLIKE SOMETHING
싶지만	"Even though I want to."	ALTHOUGH I WANT TO
힘들다	"Difficult."	TO BE DIFFICULT
괜찮다 귀찮다	"Okay, annoying, irritating."	TO BE OKAY TO BE IRRITATING

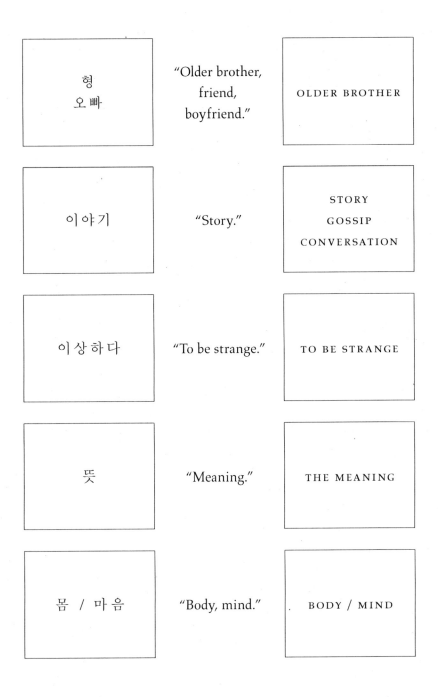

형 오빠	"Older brother, friend, boyfriend."	OLDER BROTHER
이야기	"Story."	STORY GOSSIP CONVERSATION
이상하다	"To be strange."	TO BE STRANGE
뜻	"Meaning."	THE MEANING
몸 / 마음	"Body, mind."	BODY / MIND

마음
마음씨

"Heart,
disposition."

DISPOSITION,
TEMPER

등

"Etcetera."

ETC.

농담(하다)
농담입니다

"Joke, I'm joking."

JOKE
IT'S JUST A JOKE

참다

"Like survive,
endure."

ENDURE, BEAR

빌다

"To wish."

TO WISH

피 우 다	"To start a fire."	TO MAKE A FIRE
버 리 다	"To throw away."	TO THROW AWAY
무 서 워 하 다	"To be afraid."	TO BE AFRAID
더 러 워 지 다	"To get dirty."	TO BECOME DIRTY
애 원 하 다	"To beg."	AN ENTREATY BEG

"The right person or thing." THE VERY THING/ PERSON WANTED

부재 "Absence." ABSENCE

"One more game."
"No more."
"One more."
"No. Go home."
"Last time. I promise."
Every time is the last time.

0 0 0

BREAKTHROUGH

Try telling Dr. Zhang that the breakthrough will come any day now, that it will come on network news at 6:00 and 11:00 with breaking-news music, that it will come in one-inch headlines, shrieking from the *Globe* vending machine or turned upward on the subway seat, that it will come for millions of sub-Saharan babies. Kaitlyn is trying to tell him that the breakthrough will come for her.

"It has," says Dr. Zhang. He's talking about the one-a-day pill. "Fifteen years ago, patients were taking twenty, twenty-five pills a day."

He doesn't get it, so Kaitlyn has to clarify: "That's *a* break-through, not *the* breakthrough. *A* not *the*. I'm talking about the *the*."

He closes her chart. She tells him the drug companies are only — He doesn't have time to get into it.

"Kaitlyn, it's one pill. Make your life easy — and mine — and just take the Atripla with water on an empty stomach."

000

Jeremy's good with dates, good with women too, and he's the man when dates and women coincide as they must on anniversaries, birthdays, and chick holidays. He's the man squared when it comes to serial breakups and arguments in which the girlfriend asks, *When did I say that?* Understandably, a man with such gifts for tracking time has had several epiphanies.

In the mailroom of his apartment, holding an envelope that says TIME SENSITIVE INFORMATION, Jeremy has a déjà epiphany. The actual epiphany happened three months ago, June 7, a Sunday morning, while he was watching *Faith by Feeling*. The televangelist said, "Do you believe? Do you believe? If you believe, come to the front. If you're at home and believe, raise your hand. Raise those hands high. Mmmm. Something happening in this place today, church. If you believe, touch the person next to you." So Jeremy spread his hand on the crackly TV screen and prayed that Kaitlyn wouldn't be pregnant. Then he had an epiphany, just two words long: *Get Out.* He had to, whether Kaitlyn was pregnant or not. June 7, noon, he bought three brands of pregnancy tests for her, then spent the next eight days persuading her that he was not undermining the authority of her body, nor her right to choose how her baby "communicated its presence," but simply presenting an efficient alternative to the "test of time" that involved four drops of urine on an indicator. That whole week she managed to keep him beside her or beside his phone until the ringtone conditioned Pavlovian terror in him, which made him all the more desperate to Get Out. At the mailboxes now, his whole body tenses when he recalls those wet-tissue, loose-bathrobe, bunny-slipper conversations about *what should we do? I can't kill a baby. I couldn't live with that guilt.* His talking points were simple, even simpler than Hemingway: pee + indicator = peace of mind. Finally, June 15: Negative. A respectable three weeks after the no-baby fiasco, they broke up. He changed his ringtone.

That mess happened months ago, and only now does Jeremy feel like he's recovering his old self, but a purer, refined version as only persecution can produce. At the silver mailboxes, he feels like something memorable is about to happen. September 7. Jeremy, born again of fire. Jeremy the good, the honest.

Jeremy's sure he's shining when a woman enters the mailroom. Moth to flame. He looks sideways at her mauve scrubs and asks if she's a doctor.

"No, dental hygienist."

"These days you can't tell. Doctors, nurses, hygienists, everybody's wearing — " He chins toward her outfit.

She looks down at her clothes.

He rolls his mail into a cylinder and walks to the elevator. A moment later, the hygienist is beside him, sorting through catalogues, and making little invitational moaning sounds. Inside the elevator, they chit chat mightily. She says something about wanting an LCD TV like the one in the Best Buy catalogue. He says he has one.

"Was it tough to mount?"

"Not too bad, you know. I can show it to you." He steps out and holds his palm over the elevator door.

"You mean like now?"

"It'll take two minutes."

It takes forty.

0 0 0

Arriving back at her apartment, Pony goes straight for the freezer. She digs out a spoonful of gourmet chocolate caramel ice cream, and sucks on the spoon long after she's cooled off.

0 0 0

Kaitlyn's too scared to take sleeping pills with her one-a-day, so she watches T V until she can't anymore.

But her internal narrative claims that *fear* doesn't factor into her decision not to take the pills. Rather, she's clinging to this touch of insomnia because it's her body's admirable, if misguided, struggle against sleep/death. Better, the insomnia has caused her experience of consciousness to evolve beyond the conscious/ unconscious binary into a state of being more like Buddha or Jesus, her favourite religio-tag team. Jesus is in the ring currently.

Kaitlyn's watching a late night televangelist on a high-up cable channel who is telling her that the Son of Man knows what it's like to *suffah. We oughta be glad somebody understands what it means to suffah and if we knew that, if we really knew that, church, the Lord's people would praise him more. Amen?* The praise team starts singing behind him.

Another day, another Atripla. Another day all the same.

o o o

The dental hygienist's first dates with Jeremy are homely, literally at home. She cooks for him and puts on a movie. *Homely* too in the sense that they are so wholesome they're queer. For instance, she lets him call her by her nickname, Pony, for the pet she wanted as a kid, for the hairstyle she wore through school. Sure, he could call her Pony. He wants to ride that.

But stuff like that — *Pony*, the casseroles, the movies without foul language — makes him want to handle her with two hands. And there's a whole lot more: how she worked at a grocery store from the time she was fourteen, paid her way through a two-year college, moved from some tiny central Massachusetts town to Boston, all on her own. A woman of some ambition.

A man like Jeremy, who finishes himself off as a matter of routine twice a day, what could he do with a woman like Pony, a woman his age with a modicum of principle? They hug a lot. They kiss forehead, cheek, and once lips, no tongue. They play footsies under her pies, which are made from scratch, crust and all. They say goodnight by 11:30 from opposite sides of the door. What could he do but shelve her for marriage?

After drinking each night of a long weekend, Jeremy shows up at Pony's apartment, after calling first of course, to resume his good-boy lifestyle.

"Hello yourself," Pony says. "You been out having a good time without me?" She doesn't sound jealous.

"But I've been flossing." The image of a thong rises up before him. "Here, I brought some stuff for a salad."

He also has a toolbox and a wall mount, the good kind that tilts and swivels and could support a bigger LCD TV if she decides to get one. He goes to work setting it up, ignoring Pony in the back picking through her purse and insisting she pay him back. Women love handy men, Jeremy knows. He knows she's framing the sight of him on one knee searching for a drill bit.

She brings him organic grape juice. She brings him a quartered and cored apple, locally grown. Jeremy puts a crescent in his mouth. After each offering, she stands around waiting for his approval, and Jeremy knows how to delay it until he has her in a tizzy.

He stands up suddenly.

"What do you think this is?" He pulls half his T-shirt over his head and points to his left armpit.

"Looks like a lump." Pony's hand reaches out, but stops less than an inch from it. "Does it hurt?"

Shrug. "A little."

Jeremy has been avoiding checking it out, instead telepathically consulting respected men in his life for advice: suck it up (soccer coach), wait it out (brother), walk it off (dad). To that, his father adds he hasn't been to a doctor in more than thirty years. It's not that Jeremy particularly respects Pony's medical knowledge. His slab of lean pectoral is the point here. Plus he read somewhere — no, it was Kaitlyn who told him — that a man's sweat contains pheromones that make women hum without their knowing why. Right now, with the apple response in limbo and the pheromones bombarding Pony's nervous system, she's putty.

"Do you have insurance? Do you even have a doctor, Jeremy?" Pony's concern turns him on. "It might be — "

"Might be what?" He says forlornly into his chest. He wants her to say it.

"It might be cancer."

"You think?" He puts another quarter apple in his mouth and rolls his eyes backward, in simultaneous imitation of death and orgasm. "Heaven."

"It's not. I'm just saying. Jeremy, look at me. Even if it's cancer, you could get it treated if a doctor spots it early."

If you love me. Just do it. For me. Pony says none of those things and still she gets him to go. Or that's what Jeremy wants her to think. Pony says she won't let him finish mounting the TV until he co-operates, and Jeremy protests and protests until the point of consummate pleasure then lets Pony have her way.

0 0 0

At work, it occurs to Pony that before Jeremy there was a cavity the size of a man in her.

0 0 0

Kaitlyn doesn't need a flow chart to figure out where she got it from. She's been cheated on three times that she knows of, twice by the same guy, an illegal Russian artist she rented studio space to, who has since gone back to Russia, all very suddenly, frantically, as if he were a wanted man.

After Dima, the fugitive, there was Boris, Jeremy, and Aleks, who was nothing but a rebound fling that wreaked havoc in her chakras.

The pamphlet is written in everyday language, in the spirit of "so you've got HIV," and straight-talk sex-ed documentaries. It begins, *Hello, You Are Not Alone*, then lists statistics, then, on the second flap, as part of an itemized list, it advises her to "come clean" by which it means to tell everybody who might have been exposed "unknowingly." Nicely put. But Kaitlyn finds the pamphlet neither direct in its straight talk (she is never referred to as a *killer*, for example) nor spiritually therapeutic (*You Are Not Alone* ≠ *You've Got a Friend*).

What's the protocol for coming clean? Face to face or by phone? In what order should she tell the afflicted? In the order of infection? Does the infector warrant a call? He sure as hell doesn't deserve one. Anger. Let it go. Tag Buddha, you're in. She decides to tell the only non-Russian, non-artist on the list first.

Figuring out what to say takes nights.

"I told you about a guy named Dima, right?" No.

"I tested positive." Too direct.

"My gynecologist — " Eee.

Kaitlyn doesn't know the middle part yet, but she's going to end, "You might want to get yourself checked out."

0 0 0

Jeremy applies what he learned from Kaitlyn. He rides the cancer train as long as he can. Pony runs beside it waving her handkerchief for days. Even with his mounting incomplete, and therefore his usefulness as a male asset no longer in question, he enjoys her organic grape juice, her rubbing and patting and stroking, her *poor baby* too much to rush an appointment. Once Pony became teary-eyed when they started talking about chemo. That was October 16.

The day of his appointment is marked on her calendar. October 19.

Jeremy hasn't been to Dr. Zhang since the final final pregnancy test with Kaitlyn (the three home tests, she noted, had 1–3% inaccuracy rates each, and she's always been exceptional). Jeremy finds Dr. Zhang reassuringly efficient, a hell of an engineer for a doctor. October 19, Dr. Zhang delivers his brand of no frills health care again.

"When was the last time you had a physical?"

"I can't remember."

"Are you on any drugs?"

"A multivitamin." On Pony's suggestion.

"Recreational drugs. Heroin? opiates? cocaine? marijuana?"

"I haven't smoked weed since college."

Dr. Zhang checks boxes. He frowns his loose glasses up his nose, then rolls his chair away from Jeremy.

"I'm pretty sure it's not cancer," Dr. Zhang says. "People think everything's cancer these days. Your lymph nodes are just fighting off an infection. I'll write you a prescription, keep hydrated, and you should be fine in a couple of weeks. If not, make an appointment."

He rips the prescription from the pad, rips off his gloves, disposes of them, and is at the door with Jeremy's chart flat against his pelvis before Jeremy can button his shirt.

o o o

Filling a stomach is easier than filling teeth. Pony is preparing her way to a man's heart with a dessert so sweet it'll rot a cavity into Jeremy upon contact. All the while, she's thinking about his armpit.

She answers the door in her apron.

"Well?" Pony says, helping Jeremy out of his coat.

"It's nothing, not cancer. Just something like an infected lymph node."

She crylaughs, she's so relieved, and sloshes her wet nose, her wet cheek all over his face. Then she holds him at an arm's distance.

"He gave you medication?"

"A prescription. I haven't picked it up yet."

Pony assumes her concerned tone: "Get it before this thing spreads."

000

Kaitlyn and Jeremy meet at a bar they used to visit a lot when they were dating. It's a real effort for Kaitlyn not to dole out sage pearls from her guide to enlightened living. When Jeremy says he's dying for a hot dog—a hot dog from a bar—she does not say, *Do you know what's in that?* and when she learns that Jeremy's still trying to force "small business solutions" on people working from basement home offices, she doesn't rip into him, as she used to, for being part of the corporate machinery, but mildly says, *If that's your path, Jer, then follow it.*

The hot dog arrives, smelling to Kaitlyn like the intestines of a pig, and Jeremy goes at it. She thinks it best to wait until he's done eating, but he wants to know now: Is she getting married? Is she moving? Is she a lesbian?

No.

The visible world changes key. The half-eaten hot dog bleeds on its napkin, the beer bottle weeps.

"I could give you the name of a clinic. It's that place we went to, remember? Dr. Zhang." Kaitlyn keeps trying to make things better. "It's not too far from here. You can get an appointment within a day or so."

Jeremy says nothing. Under the table their feet touch and Jeremy pulls his back quickly.

"You might be okay. It could have been Aleks after you. He cheated on me too."

Jeremy slouches back in the booth, disgust registering where his nose and cheek meet.

"I'm sorry." Kaitlyn speaks in bursts and clarifications. "It's not your fault. But it's not mine either. Suffering is always with us, underneath our happiness — that's the Buddha, not me. Jesus knew what it was like to suffer. At least somebody knows what it's like to suffer. To suffah. Sorry. Not that suffering is the take-home message out of this. It's about mindfulness. Here-and-now living. Say something."

"We almost had a kid," Jeremy says.

Again, it takes great restraint for Kaitlyn not to point out that he is misremembering. He says it like he wanted a child, like his chance to have one is gone.

o o o

Jeremy obliterates the date of Kaitlyn's confession. As far as he's concerned, it's just another workday. Not memorable. He set up a network for an immigration lawyer's office, did some troubleshooting for a layout artist/stay-at-home mom. Nothing worth remembering unless Pony shows up at his door naked under an apron.

He is watching the Bruins lose to the Rangers.

He wonders why he's not angry. He's not angry because it's not true. Plain and simple. He knows Kaitlyn. In a week, she'll have an explanation out of a theory textbook: the symptoms were just a psychosexual manifestation of her relationship with the most recent leather-clad, going-nowhere Russian artist.

To speed up the process, Jeremy plans to call her in two days and tell her he's clean. That will render her diagnosis problematic and force her into the real world where people don't go around faking pregnancies or claiming to have terminal diseases. Other people are killing themselves in hockey rinks or juggling toddlers and fledgling businesses while she's working on her drama queen routine. She's downright perverse when you think about it.

There's no way the Bruins could come back. And it's past the hour that Pony would show up with a wicked smile and a wooden spoon.

That leaves one thing. A prophylactic miracle prayer. God can't be tired of his prayer of contraception yet. Jeremy flips to a rebroadcast of *Faith by Feeling* and waits for the altar call.

o o o

The desserts seem to have worked for a while, Pony notes, but the prescription is messing up his appetite, or making him moody, or withdrawn. He has shown up at her place once in the last week and squirmed through the evening, randomly pained by certain subjects as if he were a giant sensitive tooth. For example, Pony knows better than to bring up her preemie niece again.

Pony would hate to lose the tooth. It would be harder to replace than the cavity, but ultimately less pain than living with a toothache. Easier to lose a baby than a child.

Kaitlyn's hooked on the televangelists again. She used to watch them with Jeremy, who came primed with enough Catholic guilt from childhood to render this half-an-hour penance each week. It was evangelical stuff, better than Mass, and shorter. Watching next to him, Kaitlyn could envision their kids, three of them lined up on a church pew, the boy in a suit with short pants, the two girls in hats and dresses belted with ribbon.

The televangelist says, *Lo, I'm with you always. Church you ain't hearing me this morning. My Bible says al-ways.*

The televangelist says, *Let's give Jesus a holy hand clap. For his goodness endureth forever. Let the church say,* and the church says, *Amen.*

Kaitlyn blasts the volume. When the praise team gets going, raising the roof with their hands, she says *hallelujah* in her apartment alone and stomps out a Holy Ghost dance.

The emotional high never lasts past Sunday. But then Jesus tags Buddha, and Buddha jumps in the ring.

o o o

Wait it out. Weeks go by before Jeremy actually goes for a test. Walk it off. He figures that if it was HIV, Dr. Zhang would have known from the lump. Suck it up. And lumps are more of a cancer-related symptom in any case.

Jeremy will remember Dr. Zhang as looking fat and tired that day, November 12. Disappointed too, like he was suffering from erectile dysfunction.

Contracted, he says with Jeremy's chart in front of him. Then Jeremy can't hear what he's saying anymore. *Contracted.* Today is November 12. The doctor's eyebrows go up. His hands play an invisible accordion. He searches along the shelves for something, then produces a brochure—no kidding—and hands it to Jeremy. His latex-free gloves stay on the whole time. Today is November 12. Jeremy's good with dates.

Appointment to talk to someone is what Jeremy manages to reconstruct from the last sounds he hears. He nods. He says he will call someone to set something up sometime, and Dr. Zhang is out the door before Jeremy can extend his hand.

Sealed airtight in his car, in traffic, inundated with soft rock, Jeremy tries to rip off the steering wheel. *Give me the cancer. I want the cancer.*

o o o

Pony is pacing in her apartment wearing tights with stirrups, head cocked intimately into the cordless, waiting for Jeremy to pick up. She wants to take their relationship, as people on TV say, to the next level, or possibly a base closer to home (home = marriage; this is softball, not baseball), but she's not sure how to broach the issue without being indelicate. It is the man's job after all to initiate advances, and the woman's to set the pace of that progress by her refusals and permissions.

She has selected a romantic comedy with Jennifer Aniston for tonight. If that doesn't put Jeremy in the mood to discuss being in a committed but lighthearted relationship, filled with witty banter and grand epiphanies, then her name isn't Pony.

Jeremy's not answering his phone. She'll leave another message.

o o o

"I'm clean," Jeremy's voice says.

/ 59 /

Kaitlyn says she's happy for him. And she is, she is. It's just that when she and her sister had chicken pox together, they were quarantined in their shared room with a clock radio and a box of old *National Geographics*. She was hoping for something like that again.

A few weeks later, while Kaitlyn is making an egg white mask, Jeremy calls again.

"It showed up."

So completely has she dismissed the possibility that she has to ask, "What?"

"What you got."

She stops stirring. None of the other men so much as returned her call, and she was forced into the ethical corner of having to leave a message on their voicemails. She figured she was in this alone, so she has nothing prepared to say to Jeremy.

"Did they give you the brochure?"

"Christ, Kaitlyn. I've got this girl I'm gonna marry."

That Wednesday, Kaitlyn and Jeremy meet at the same bar, same corner booth. He leans across the table and whispers angrily at her for twenty minutes. She spends the next half hour telling him that the disease is not what it was in the 80s or 90s, not an immediate death sentence, that philosophically they are no different from anyone on the earth, just enlightened about the time of their passing, that partners stay together, that there are many herbal remedies to boost the immune system, that if he listens to his body it will tell him what it needs.

From then on, every Wednesday after work, the two of them quarantine themselves in that booth. Soft rock going in the background, printouts from the Internet, same faces working the shift.

000

After mounting the TV, Jeremy increases the memory of Pony's computer, helps her set up a new dining table, and builds her a twenty-four-bottle spice carousel for Christmas, irrefutably establishing his manhood. After that, Jeremy cuts back on spending time with her. He has stuff to take care of. That's what he says verbatim, "stuff to take care of," which comes out sounding unintentionally harsh.

He's taking Kaitlyn's advice, which is to concentrate on himself for a while, specifically on wellness, holistic health, not on beating the disease. She becomes his guru. "The body has no name for what's happening inside, but it knows how to fight the disease better than any MD."

Jeremy finds Kaitlyn's enthusiasm contagious. She's into these miracle cures — "they're not miracle cures; they're herbal remedies" — although she abandons them every three weeks or so. "Not right for my body." She's even been to a faith healer who hosts a series of evangelistic meetings in Worcester. Nothing. Still, every time she talks about a new discovery, a breakthrough, Jeremy plays the role of skeptic until Kaitlyn's defense reaches a feverish pitch, then he douses her with belief.

Because he wants to believe her, because believing her would mean hope for his own situation, Jeremy is in the bathtub inhaling from Kaitlyn's bottle of eucalyptus oil, "an immunostimulant." The eucalyptus is new for her, but he knows, from the time they were together, that she's into long baths. Jeremy would find a knife and piece of cucumber in their last positions on the counter, and the containers of oatmeal and honey, taken directly into the bathroom, sitting on the toilet seat. And if it wasn't oatmeal, honey, and cucumber, it was milk and green tea or ginger and orange peel. She wasn't a soap and water woman.

He mocked her baths then, but now he's watching his knees

form islands in diluted tomato juice, "lycopene for the prostate," ginger "for blood flow," and a carton of blueberries, "powerful antioxidants," which he's afraid will stain the bathtub. The water goes cold. The blueberries float like goat turds.

Jeremy tries the baths. He tries a tea of traditional Chinese herbs. He tries sprinkling turmeric on his food. He tries taking milk thistle for his liver. He tries his best. And he feels no different from his June 7, September 7, November 12 selves.

o o o

The movies without cussing pile up on top of Pony's DVD player and she watches them hungrily on the weekends, all in a Friday/ Saturday binge, eating shepherd's pie straight from the dish, weeping on her sleeve for the heroines.

o o o

Kaitlyn knows that the Coke in front of Jeremy is only to forestall a lecture on the well-documented dangers of alcohol, part 3. Her cup of hot water arrives. She pours out some MegaImmune from a vial in her bag, covers the cup with an ashtray, and waits.

"You have to keep doing it," Kaitlyn says from her side of the booth. Not that she's one to talk, queen of consistency.

As unofficial lifestyle and enlightenment counsellor, Kaitlyn notes Jeremy's progress in accepting what he's been dealt. The first few Wednesdays they met, he'd answer, "Fine," before she could finish asking, "How do you feel?" Then they'd talk about common acquaintances, his job, and at the end, after a long silence, he'd begin, "You know," then throw out a paragraph about this disease, which he never names, but calls, "this disease" not his, not hers, not ours, but *this* — between them right then, as real as the ashtray or the hot sauce.

Their quarantine Wednesdays are free of sexual energy, at least from Kaitlyn's side. They talk as if their history is well behind them, as if they are on the other side of *someday you're going to laugh about this*. Jeremy tells Kaitlyn his side of the baby fiasco, about the ringtone. He tells her all about Pony and the videos, the apron, the salads.

"Have you told her yet?" Kaitlyn asks, as she does each week.

Then suddenly that relationship also becomes platonic.

We're friends, really good friends / It's impossible to go to the next level / I can't mess up what we've got now / I'm real careful around her so there's no real risk / She'd just worry herself to death.

"The longer you wait, the more explaining you'll have to do," Kaitlyn says. "Even as friends."

The waitress takes Jeremy's bottle by the neck and walks away, wagging her printed bottom, *SHORTY'S*. Jeremy's eyes are two palms on her cheeks.

"I missed that. What'd you say?" Jeremy says.

He'd sooner die of celibacy than this disease.

o o o

Looking at *SHORTY'S* walk away, Jeremy sees the end of Mardi Gras (February 28), spine-spasming (July 27), major leg-cramping (March 13), upside down (November 11), drunken stranger (April 19, June 3, December 31), record-breaking marathon (May 22), makeup (October-November), soap slippery (mornings, January), down and dirrrty (May 22), operatic (May 22), chocolate syrup and whipped creamy (May 22), drywall-busting (May 22), role playing

(October 28), Batman costumed (October 31), tied-up-and-gagged (July 5), outdoor (August 18), unprotected (off and on), pony-riding (   ) sex.

o o o

With her mask on and her patient more or less asleep, Pony's thoughts slip to Jeremy.

She thinks she's getting fat. He must have noticed how much she likes to eat. Men don't like — what does she know about what men don't like? Men don't like getting nowhere.

"Open a little wider."

Maybe she isn't nice enough. Be sweeter, which means giving Jeremy whatever he wants. If he wants his space, she'll disappear. If he wants to see her, she'll stop what she's doing. These are short-term sacrifices.

"Open some more."

But she knows what the problem is — she's heard it from other men. She's a prude, she's a square, an uptight goody goody, a waste of a body, a spinster in waiting. Even her father would threaten to cut her ponytail while she slept. In this decade, what are homemade pies and PG-13 movies?

"Turn to your left."

She should learn to talk dirty, find reason to model a frilly red teddy. She should rent him porn. *Gross*, she thinks, she can't help it. But dirty talk, she could start practicing with this patient. *Which part of me do you want in your mouth? Do you ever fantasize about a girl in uniform, Mr. Mussman? I bet you could show me how a guy likes his instrument handled.* Oh, she's no good at it.

"Have a rinse and spit in the bowl."

As he's coming into the pub with a fake redhead, one of Jeremy's colleagues spots Jeremy and Kaitlyn in the corner booth. He comes over to show off the redhead, who's taller, skinnier, toothier, breastier than Kaitlyn. Everybody knows it, especially Big Red, who Kaitlyn sizes up competitively. Strike *competitively*. Kaitlyn would call that look *pitying*, because Big Red has no idea that she's setting back the movement.

"Pearls." Kaitlyn says. That's Big Red's language.

"You like them?"

"Classy."

Then the next three things that happen are like the backswing of a demolition ball through the evening: Jeremy gets a call and slides out of the booth to take it; Colleague ushers Big Red into Jeremy's side of the booth then sits down next to her; Big Red leans over so her breasts are pressed against the table, presumably to show Kaitlyn the pearls up close.

"Cla-ssy," says Kaitlyn into her drink.

"Man, he's looking good," Colleague says.

Kaitlyn glances at Jeremy as he walks away. "Like a cross between JFK and Elvis. The hair. I tell him he's — "

"He must have lost five, ten pounds."

"clogging his scalp," Kaitlyn rolls on, "with all of that product."

"Wish I could drop a few."

"You must have him on a diet," Big Red says, straight out of the fifties.

Kaitlyn turns to Big Red. "I don't believe in diets. I believe in — "

"I think you two must have a pretty strenuous workout," Colleague says, fondling Big Red's shoulder.

"informed eating decisions. As with anything,"

"Could be lipo," says Big Red with her high fifties voice.

"consciousness is the key. You just need to be mindful of"

"I'll put twenty bucks on lipo," says Big Red.

"what you put in your mouth, what you put in your body. You know, refuse "

"Lipo? Men don't get lipo. That's some good ol' fashioned lovin' right there."

"to be a consumer on autopilot."

"Yeah, yeah, down with corporations. What's the deal with Jeremy?" Colleague says. "We have a bet going here."

"HIV," Kaitlyn says.

Colleague and Big Red laugh through their noses. Seeing that Kaitlyn's not laughing, Colleague says, "You're joking, right?"

They don't know her well enough to be sure.

000

When Jeremy comes back to the booth, Colleague and Big Red take long sips of their drinks.

"That was Pony. She's working till seven."

"Pony?" Colleague says.

"Yeah, she's my — I guess you could say she's my — "

"I thought you two were together," Colleague says, pointing at Kaitlyn and Jeremy. "I'm sorry, what's your name again, hon?"

Kaitlyn tells him reluctantly.

"Kaitlyn, that's right." Then he addresses Jeremy, as if the women can't hear. "She's the sauce on the side. Gotcha."

Everyone laughs except Kaitlyn. Big Red leans low into the table and Jeremy cops a glance at her unruly breasts.

000

"Open up."

No one has asked Pony yet, *What happened to that guy you met, that guy who put up your* TV? But it will come, and when it does, she'll have to pretend she hasn't thought of him: *Who, Jeremy? You know, I don't know. I should give him a call. I guess he's still around, but we don't see each other much. I try to pick up some extra hours when I can, and he's probably swamped too.*

"You haven't been brushing well or flossing."

And what's he been doing all these evenings? Drinking on the weekends, eating tuna from the can and pickles from the bottle. He's so hopeless. She remembers he didn't know how to clean and season chicken, and forget having him dice garlic. He couldn't slice a tomato in its proper orientation, could barely wash lettuce clean. *Rinsing is not washing,* she had to tell him.

"It looks like this bleeding you're having might be gingivitis."

These days she's packing herself peanut butter sandwiches and yogurt for lunch. No sense cooking big meals anymore. She'd end up eating the same creamy chicken enchiladas for three days. She doesn't mind the food; it's just the ache of reheating, of pressing the microwave buttons evening after evening, eating from plastic containers and watching the TV Jeremy put up without turning it on.

"I'll have Dr. O'Connor check you for cavities when I'm done."

0 0 0

Outside the bar with Jeremy, Kaitlyn has twisted a simple question —Big Red's breasts, real or fake?—into a colloquium on whether the contemporary breast is a maternal, tactile, or aesthetic object. Kaitlyn says the sexual aura in the booth was toxic: Big Red's look-but-don't-touch breasts, Colleague's latent homosexuality.

"Back up. What?"

"You know I'm tolerant and everything, but the guy was practically shagging you with his eyes all evening."

"Please."

"When Pony called and you left, you should have heard him. 'Oh, his hair. Oh, his body. Oh, he's so thin.' I had to tell him. As if he heard a word I said!"

Jeremy stops walking. From behind her, he says, "Tell him what?"

"Oh, Jeremy, come on." Kaitlyn says. "Don't play naïve." She turns to face him.

"You told him I had," he looks around, then drops his voice to a stage whisper, "this disease?"

"I told him the truth. He wanted the truth. I gave it to him."

"You know that's not all you did."

"I have stopped living in shame, Jeremy."

"Did you tell him about you? Huh?"

"He didn't ask about me, but I would have. You have a responsibility to the people in your life. To tell them."

"One more time. Tell me your exact words." Jeremy paces in a circle. The sidewalk is empty. He puts his hands behind his head and looks up. Before Kaitlyn can answer, he says, "You know what? I just have to get another job. Eight years in the garbage."

"Don't be rash." Kaitlyn tells him he needs to locate the courage to tell the people close to him.

"I work with this guy, Kaitlyn. I have to see him every day."

"Then he's there for you."

"He's there for me! He's there for me!" Jeremy kicks dust at her. "Who is there for anybody? Who's there for you? You're dead."

The news enters Kaitlyn visibly, as if she were swallowing it rather than hearing it.

(The next quarantine Wednesday, she doesn't show up.)

"I'll have a Heineken," Jeremy tells the bartender. Same night, different bar. Where no one knows his name.

As he sees it, he has two options. A) February 3: the day Kaitlyn ruined his career. Or B) February 3: the bender to end all benders. He opts for B and rolls his sleeves over his elbows — business to be done — in preparation for a transfusion of beer and Russian vodka. He orders a basket of chicken wings, because he needs to tear something apart (Kaitlyn's limbs, no fancy psychoanalysis there) with his teeth.

The pre-game Heineken arrives, and he drains it before the wings arrive. Bruins are on. And tonight, damn it, they're going to win.

The wings arrive. Ring her neck right off, that's what he's going to do. Jeremy goes through the wings with a predator's enthusiasm. (He'll have to play Kaitlyn's comment as a joke, frame her as having an "unusual sense of humour." It's the only way. Find a job in this economy? She may have screwed him for a good two years.) He orders another Heineken.

"Come on, that was a penalty!" Jeremy shouts up at the wall-mounted TV. (Wall mount → Pony → Pony! Kaitlyn has screwed him for life.) His second beer arrives.

He breaks every bone in each chicken wing, alternating wishes between *breakthrough cure* and *dead Kaitlyn*. When that's done, he takes to screaming at the television. A third beer. Fourth. Fifth. The bar crowd is getting uneasy with him.

"Take it easy, cowboy."

"Trying to watch the game here."

"Spoiled college kids."

It's that last comment from a squeaky-voiced black guy that pisses Jeremy off because he is *not* spoiled. He's been working since he was fourteen, he believes by beer six, at a grocery store in some tiny central Massachusetts town and put himself through a bloody two-year college to become a dental hygienist.

Jeremy walks over to the skinny black guy, who's in his forties, and says, "You want a piece of me?"

Although he's never been in a fist fight in his life, Jeremy plans to wallop this guy until his knuckles are bleeding then fist his mouth roughly for talking trash about someone who's just unwinding after a bad day with some chicken wings and beer, but instead is led out into an adjoining parking lot and beaten so soundly that when he wakes up he has to crawl around the asphalt to find his phone.

He is trying to remember the date to attach to this event and finds that he can't.

000

Pony's at home, of course.

"Pony," Jeremy sings. Something's wrong with the connection. "Pooony."

"Jeremy?" She's never heard him like this.

"How come you don't call me cowboy?" Jeremy says.

"Jeremy, I thought we were going to — "

"No. Cowboy. Call me cowboy."

"Okay, cowboy, what happened?"

"Because I'm your cowboy. I'm your cowboy, Pony. You know I'm your cowboy. Say it. I'm your cowboy. I'm your boy, Pony. I'm your" and the rest disintegrates into babbling.

"You're my cowboy." Pony's apartment goes blurry.

"I have no money, Pony. I spent all my money. Can't find my keys. I'm bleeding. I'm too bloody drunk to be with you."

Her apartment dissolves.

"I'm too bad to drive. I need a ride. Can you hear me?"

Pony figures out that he's made his way to the steps of an elementary school ten minutes from their building.

"Stay where you are."

"You're the best. I don't deserve you." He's breaking up. "Really, I'm [   ], Pony."

She fills in *in love with you*, gets dressed, and sets out.

o o o

A couple of weeks go by, and Kaitlyn's back for quarantine Wednesday with news for Jeremy, a revelation, a breakthrough. He rolls his coat into the corner of the booth and sits down heavily.

"Where were you last week?" he asks.

"In the hospital, but you're not going to believe this."

"Wait. Hospital?"

"Uh huh." Kaitlyn pauses a moment. Jeremy opens his eyes wide. "You remember that place I went to in Worcester—"

"Why were you in the hospital?" Jeremy shakes his head. "Are you all right?"

"Listen. After I went to that healer in Worcester, I thought to myself I need to give myself completely to his plan, not *his* plan, but *a* plan, *a* not *his*, have full faith in something if I expect it to work, so I quit taking my meds."

"You did what?"

"*Listen.* I stopped taking my meds like three weeks ago. I said no more of this for me. I'm tired of pills—sleeping pills, Aspirin, Atripla, pills, pills, pills. I'm tired of the pharmaceutical companies telling me I need pills. Up till last week I was feeling okay, then I started feeling out of breath and crampy all the time, and I passed out."

"When was this, exactly?"

"Last Monday. The ambulance came and everything. My viral count was at 100, 000."

Jeremy repeats the number. He knows what it means. Anything over 40, 000 and she should be dead.

"So I spent three days in Intensive Care, comatose. Doctor said I had days to live" — Kaitlyn laughs — "and look, I'm here with you. But you know what happened when I went under, there in Intensive Care? I knew something bad was happening, because there was a light. A light. I had to shade my eyes like, and at the end of the light there was this silhouette of a man. I knew right away who it was. Nobody has to tell you."

Kaitlyn spreads both her hands wide, her fingers exploding outwards.

Jeremy's frown deepens.

"Jesus. I saw Jesus. And he's beautiful, let me tell you. He's so beautiful. I said *Jesus* and he said back to me, talking just like you and me here, *Kaitlyn, you're healed.* And I felt — it's hard to explain — like I was in warm water, like standing up after a bath when all the water is running off you. Best way I can describe it is like floating in amniotic fluid, then it breaks and washes over you and then you're born. When I woke up the two nurses were crying. After that my viral count

o o o

dropped to 80, 000," Kaitlyn finishes up.

Jeremy's neck is craned forward. He's frowning painfully. He wants her to say exactly what she's suggesting.

"So..." he wafts a hand for the conclusion.

"I believe I'm cured," Kaitlyn says.

Jeremy, like the nurses, like the doctors, asks the wrong thing first.

"Cured?" he asks.

Kaitlyn nods. "He that believeth in me shall not perish."

They should ask, *You believe*

000

that guy?" Jeremy says to Pony as she helps him into her apartment, through the dim foyer, with her head under his arm. "He's a punk. And you know what I am?"

"You're a cowboy," Pony says. They've had this conversation about eight times between the parking lot and her bedroom.

"That's right."

Pony drops him heavily on the bed onto his back. From the knee up his body assumes the position of a cross; his feet remain on the floor. His mouth relaxes into sleep. Pony unrolls his socks, then unbuttons his shirt tenderly. She has to use all her strength to lift the dead weight of his torso to get the shirt off. She loosens his belt, unbuttons his waist, checks — yes he's wearing boxers — and, standing at his feet, drags his pants off.

All Pony wants is to keep him — with his jaw of brown stubble and his slowly dying front tooth. He smells damp, sweaty, and fermented. In his left armpit, the lump is still there, meaning, to Pony after too many weekends of melodramatic movie plotlines, that all these months, all this time Jeremy's been avoiding her was because of this tumour, a malignant, inoperable tumour. He drinks himself to death the nights he's not at her place.

She lies flat on the bed next to him, her head resting on one of his arms, hands on her stomach, eyes closed. Sometime in the night he turns and puts his other arm around her

MegaImmune vial is filled with Kaitlyn's blood (she talked a nurse into giving it to her as a souvenir) and she wears it around her neck. She leans over to show Jeremy, as Big Red did two weeks ago.

"It's the blood of Jesus."

Jeremy doesn't seem impressed. "What if it wasn't Jesus?"

"Who healed me?" Kaitlyn washes her fries in ketchup. "If a kingdom be divided against itself, that kingdom cannot stand." Then she adds as a flourish, "Mark 3:24."

The size of Kaitlyn's meal seems straight out of Texas, and from the looks of it she will eat every last french fry.

Jeremy doesn't let the point drop. "I mean what if you didn't see God? Like, say, you saw someone else."

"The devil? But I'm healed."

"What if he lied to you?"

o o o

The next morning, February 4, Jeremy wakes up. Pony wakes up. She makes him breakfast, packs him lunch, like man and wife.

o o o

Six months later.
Not yet.

o o o

Six months later.

Not yet.

000

Six months later.

000

BREAK-IN

Hoop planned to get in and out as quickly as possible. Six to eight
minutes is all it should take to storm a house. Treat it like a timed
shopping spree, like a game show, like a shot clock speeding to
0:00 at the top of the screen. But the back bedroom with its otherworldly girliness threw him, and when he heard the garage door
rumbling up, he ran down the stairs, then down one more level
(he panicked) into the basement and hid under the stairs. He didn't
even see the side entrance.

Late evening, a month into first semester, a guy and his girl walk
from school to Phase 2 of The Houses. He leads her to a Siamese
house, joined at the cheek. He leads her to the left twin and they
enter through the mouth. Inside is a mess of exposed plumbing,
wood, and wires. Orange codes are spray-painted on the walls.

He's been in houses like this before, in this situation or nearly.

This house—this whole subdivision—was five stops from Hoop's aging apartment complex. The balconies of his building were streaked with rust. So he was attracted to the new development, and from the back corner seat of the 41 bus, he tracked its progress over the spring like a seed growing in a paper cup. First the land was bulldozed, then mixer trucks planted cement into the patterns of an old civilization, then workers put up wooden walls, then plastic walls, then dark shingles, then various colours of brick. By the end of April some of the houses were almost ready to be occupied. Hoop—not for Hooper, but for his skills balling—and his friend Duane got off the bus early to explore what guys were calling, with bravado, The Houses.

Everyone knew that guys took girls to The Houses to get some, except for the ninth graders, who still preferred the mall for soft-core, handholding, closed-mouthed action.

The day Hoop and Duane first explored The Houses, the front door of lot 23L was unlocked. There were beige ceramic tiles in the small front foyer, and a step up to a narrow hallway, then, in walking sequence, powder room, basement door, open-concept kitchen (with breakfast bar), dining and family rooms, and a small raised deck beyond the sliding glass patio doors.

The guy suggests they use the basement to avoid curious home-owners or kids looking for hide-and-seek territory. Those types usually stay on the main floor, or they go upstairs and check out the bedrooms.

"No one ever goes down to the basement," he says. What's there to see? Insulation, concrete floors, a drain, bare bulbs, support beams, maybe a rough-in for a bathroom.

"Look at this," Duane said. He was still at the entrance, one hand on the door, the other on the frame. "All you gotta do is knock and the whole thing'll fly apart."

"What are you talking about?" Hoop walked back to the foyer.

Duane closed the door and turned the lock. "See how this deadbolt fits in here? The casing — the wood — all around the frame is really thin. The only thing holding it there is these nails. What? Half inch?"

"'Cause of the glass," Hoop said. There were panels on either side of the door, so the lock was barely longer than the door latch.

"Yeah. They can't nail the casing in any more." Duane pulled hard on the locked door and the frame seemed to give. "They best get an alarm up in here."

0 0 0

At the time *Not at night* At the time *Better in the afternoon when everyone's at work* Hoop had no plans to invade lot 23L *Dress normal — a hoody or a jersey and nobody'll look at you twice* But that little piece of information from Duane *With all the Blacks and Indians in the area you'll just look like somebody's kid* existed for

Close to her ear, he says, "We could get our *mmm* on down here" and puckers his lips slightly, cool, touches the brim of his hat.

She knows this is where girls come to let themselves be touched. The fur around her hood dusts her forehead. She's been to The Houses before, not since Phase I though, and then it wasn't with this guy.

Hoop *Who knows his neighbour anymore* like a theory to be proven *Bring a package, ring the doorbell, enter through the door inside the garage* But if it were possible simply to enter a house by kicking down the door *Easy as that* why weren't more houses robbed *Think of the cred, man* or why weren't more people robbing their neighbours?

Bus ride after bus ride *Only bag stuff small enough to fit in a knapsack* the thought swelled in his head *and not too much, laptop, MP3 player, camera* until he finally *If it don't fit you must acquit* finally he

o o o

tried to get in and out as quickly as possible. Six to eight minutes is enough to take. With seven minutes left, Hoop saw photos over the fireplace. To blue eyes, the girls in separate frames might look like the same girl or twins: each wore two thick plaits like upside down horns on the side of her head, a toothless thick-lipped smile, the same pink sweater though the turtlenecks worn underneath were different. But he could tell that they were not the same girl, not twins either. Just poor, at the time, and wearing hand-me-downs.

He makes a show of opening the basement door for her. She steps down carefully, holding her hair to the sides of her face. Behind her, the guy's arms swish against his bubble vest. This morning he only had style in mind, but during the last two afternoon periods, when he proposed the idea of hanging out after school, the vest turned into something else — padding.

Six left. Hoop saw a glasses case and telephone bill on the arm of the converted patio chair in the family room. The surname on the envelope was Pearson, like the airport.

Five left. Upstairs in the master bedroom, he caught himself, knapsack on one shoulder, in the mirror of the ensuite. On the counter, a bottle of baby oil, a tube of cut-open foundation, and a comb with hair curling in it stared back at him like three guard dogs. He heard for the first time the low growl of the refrigerator downstairs.

Four left. He arrived in the otherworldly back bedroom, the older girl's, wallpapered with posters, carpeted with skirts and dresses left where she stepped out of them. Three left, he didn't know what to take. His bag was still empty. Three left. He heard the 41 pass. Three left. He found an MP3 player with headphones still attached on the bed. Two left. The garage door opened. Two left. He inadvertently ran to the basement. Two left. The car doors closed. There should be two minutes left. He ducked his head under the comforter covering boxes under the stairs. Overtime.

For a gun he had a boxcutter.

0 0 0

Light slants downward through the small windows on one side of the basement. Flecks of dust turn somersaults in the smoky light. The girl started talking dirty into his ear during third or fourth period, and now she wishes she hadn't. In this hollowed house, its ribs showing like the inside of a cathedral or a half-eaten turkey, she feels both watched and abandoned.

Hoop was already hoping for an inaccurate suspect description, for a neighbour to say, *male black six feet between twenty and twenty-five at least two hundred pounds dark baggy clothes baseball cap with a hood pulled over it.* And that wouldn't be Hoop. He looked eighteen but was fifteen, black yes, tall yes, not wearing what she saw, but an oversized basketball jersey. He was long-necked and his arms had the definition of a woman who curled light weights.

And he was strong, though he didn't look it. Shaking his hand or escaping his headlock, you'd wonder where he stored all that strength. His bones must be made of metal.

o o o

Whatever happened upstairs happened in Hoop's head.

"Some wayward boy do this," the woman said. Her deep voice engorged Hoop's heart with rhythm. *Wayward* was his mother's word.

"Call the police." A teenaged voice.

"Him gone."

"Call the police. Don't touch anything. He could come back. What if he's still here?"

The patio door slid open.

"Let's go upstairs," she says, turning around with her arms folded.

"Hold up, hold up," he says. He takes both her hands in his, unfolds her arms. "Didn't you say you wanted—"

"It's dirty."

"Dirty, huh." He speaks into her lips. "You been talking dirt all day."

"Tasha. Tasha! Stay here."

Pattering, then a child's voice: "I wasn't going anywhere."

"Hello? Somebody break in my house. (From the mother's responses, Hoop could tell what the dispatcher was asking.) I'm at 12 Deerpass Lane. It don't have a number outside, lot 23L. [←Where do you live?] In the kitchen. [←Where are you now?] No, my two girls with me. [←Are you alone?] I don't know. I don't see anybody. The door was open when I come home. [←Is the suspect there?] The front door. [←Which door did you find open?] No, like the inside door from the garage. Him kick it down. [←The front door?] Please send somebody quick, the police. I live at twel— [←The officers will be there any minute.] I didn't look. I don't know. [←Is anything missing?] I think so. We in the kitchen. [←Are you all safe?] Okay. Okay. Mm. Okay. [←Here's what I want you to do…]."

There's no reason to be afraid of me, Hoop thought downstairs. He was a spider at the heel of a woman. *Three* females. It might be better to get out now, just run, up the stairs, out the front, wave the boxcutter. He could cover his face. When the police came, there'd be no waving the boxcutter. Lord Jesus. Straight to Juvy. And his mother. Lord God.

Isn't anything he says that makes her stay—he could have been on mute—but strobe flashes of him on the court with his wifebeater pulled up behind his neck, and his slow kiss near her locker, thumb on her chin, and girls everywhere razing her with their eyes. This guy was—*real* was the only word, so said his shining bottom lip, his peach breath, and hot hands. She would approach the next few minutes as a job to be done, a vegetable to be eaten.

"Police!" Boots clomped overhead.

"In the kitchen," said the mother, Ms. (there was no man on the mantle) Pearson.

In Hoop's head, and possibly upstairs, the officers were wearing fatigues and Stallone headbands. One of them, Goliath-sized, spoke mechanically into his shoulder-mounted walkie-talkie, which beeped back before emitting a voice hoarse with static. Another officer, shorter, unable to grow facial hair, wearing a too-big uniform, and carrying a bazooka, appeared behind the first like an echo. Goliath told Ms. Pearson and her girls to wait where they were. He told his walkie-talkie, not the family, that he had already searched the first floor, that Echo was proceeding into the basement, and that he would search upstairs.

Echo never seemed to be looking at anything in particular. His gaze darted around as if tracking a housefly. The kind of man who snaps. The soldier cops walked around, touching boxes on their hips or shoulders, and Ms. Pearson stood at a distance inside her house, as if it were the model, open for the public to inspect, to walk on the carpet in dirty shoes. At that moment, Hoop wanted Goliath slain and Echo silenced, for what they had turned her house into.

o o o

If she feels like it later she might talk to her girls — her real girls — that night. Right now, she doesn't think she'll feel like it.

He, on the other hand, has a breathy re-enactment all set for tomorrow: *She was like* Oh no no, *and I was like Yeas,* No oh, *Yeas,* Noh, *Yeeas,* Oh yeaaas yes!

He only kneads her body for a few minutes. Then it starts to relax.

Every sense shut off except Hoop's hearing. First he heard footsteps descending, each foot a different pitch. The melody made him want to cry. The footsteps belonged to Echo — Echo in his fatigues of a thousand pockets, something deadly in each, bazooka cocked over his shoulder, hand gun held sideways, little red laser searching for Hoop's black forehead.

Then Hoop heard Echo pull a chain. He was so well-covered that he did not notice the light. Or were his eyes closed?

Next rubber across the floor. That was the cold cellar opening. Another chain being pulled. On then off. The door closed.

The feet passed him. The washer opened. The dryer. On the way back to the stairs, the footsteps stopped. The officer knocked some boxes under the stairs with his gun, then again with the bazooka. He was waiting for the thief to screw things up, to sneeze or cough or shuffle. Hoop thought his trembling was seismic. Wasn't he panting? Wasn't his heart drumming? He knew this story from Poe and Lisa Simpson. Now was the time to burst through the boxes, screaming something, throwing his backpack at the feet of the officer, compressing the sides of his head between his hands.

0 0 0

His cue comes from her knees, which bounce slowly as if in a pool, then her legs give way. He spits out his gum and kisses her neck, the side of her face. One of her hands slides on the bubble vest beneath her, the other pushes against his shoulder. Something feels sharp, the vest's zipper, maybe a loose nail. She thinks, irrationally and maybe foolishly, but she thinks it all the same: *I don't want to die like this.*

Whatever happened upstairs seemed to happen far away in a smoky, tropical place. Hoop saw them all standing ankle-deep in swampy water.

Goliath got Ms. Pearson's story. She was questioned only for information, as if her fear and sense of violation were extravagances. The girls didn't say anything. They just stood to one side of their mother in descending height, partially obscured by palm fronds. The older one watched the officer drill her mother first with his mouth, then with his eyes, then with something further back in his skull like a low frequency wave.

After each question, Hoop could fill in what Goliath was thinking.

Do you own this home? [←She's probably renting. We should speak to the owners.]

You were all off the premises — [←Dumb down your language, boy.] You were out shopping, you said, when the break-in occurred?

No one saw the suspect. True? [←Black on black crime.]

Goliath studied the woman's hairline. *Unsure*, he wrote, just to write something. He studied the curtains hanging by thumbtacks, the cushions on patio furniture, and wrote *new owners*.

Were these rooms empty before? [←What do you have to steal?]

He backs away suddenly and sits on his heels, fumbling with his zipper now instead of with her. She distracts herself. Where did his hat go? Wasn't he wearing a hat?

He is saying something, but he is on mute again, reaching for his wallet. The sight of it, thick and brown, tips her mind. She looks at the wad of gum on the cement floor.

"Won't hurt."

Echo had been wading in circles around the kitchen, looking for that housefly. After a few moments, he announced his intention (to his walkie-talkie) to search the exterior of the premises.

The patio door opened and closed. Through a nearby basement window, Hoop saw Echo's combat boots walk back and forth. From the attitude of the boots, Hoop guessed Echo was smoking.

He heard, "Not much furniture. Looks like she was robbed before," followed by a rush of air out Echo's nostrils, not a laugh quite. And, most significantly, he heard a smile on the other end of the walkie-talkie.

o o o

When the police left, the upstairs part of the house started to collapse like a deflating air mattress. The conversation was flimsy and tremulous. Tasha didn't have to sleep alone if she didn't want to. The door from the garage needed to be secured until they could change the lock. The thug could come back. The thugs. A gang of them.

A moment after he tears open the package and unrolls the rubber the upstairs door opens. Footsteps patter. A woman's voice, *Too small, this foyer, but look they have a step up to the hallway.* The girl pulls her clothes close to her, straightens up. The guy stops her arm. No sound. *Oh and Kevin look at this kitchen, see I told you the island was necessary, and look looklooklooklook they upgraded the backsplash.*

He heard things being moved. Perhaps the Pearsons were making old-fashioned booby traps. Cans and bottles by the front foyer. A houseplant by the patio door.

Hoop looked at the time on his cell phone. 6:58. He'd been in the basement for hours, and he had hours more to go before the family went to sleep. When they were all in the bedrooms, he'd sneak out. Except for his knees, which had been too sharply bent for too long, he was fairly comfortable under the stairs. Earlier, he had completely removed the comforter from over his head so that his eyes could get adjusted to the dark. But there was nothing to see.

Upstairs, they were watching TV. Drawers and cupboards closed. The music for an entertainment tabloid came on.

"Ready," the mother called over the music. "Tasha, come and eat."

Hoop smelled fried sardines upstairs. He was hungry, and gassy. That was another reason he uncovered his head.

"Did they check the cold room in the basement?" Ms. Pearson asked.

The voices continue upstairs into the bedrooms. In the basement, the guy and the girl look upward, as if listening with their eyes.

When the voices finally leave, the girl says with her palms, *I can't do this. It's too risky.*

"They're gone," he says, but she is already off his vest, brushing shavings from her skirt.

"I don't know. You want me to go down?" The older girl volunteered herself. "Give me a broom or something."

"You don't have to go. Eat." Ms. Pearson sucked her teeth. "I thought I heard—It's the neighbour maybe. They build these houses too close."

"You can use my umbrella," said Tasha.

"Girl, go and sit down!" Ms. Pearson said. "That's your food from this morning."

"I'll check," said the teenaged voice.

The basement light went on. Through the slats in the stairs, Hoop saw her ripple down: one dry bare heel then another, the back of her knee, the fingers of one hand around a yellow and red, Pooh umbrella, the other hand must have been on the banister. She reached the bottom, and, like Echo, walked to the cold room.

"I don't see anything," she shouted up as if checking the hold of a grappling hook.

"Hurry up," a little voice came back.

Ms. Pearson: "Girl, don't make me talk to you again. Sit. Down."

"I said I can't, all right." She starts up the stairs. "Don't follow me right away."

No answer.

"I'll meet you by the site office."

"Whatever."

She squeezes her chin into her neck and looks down on him from the basement stairs. His boxers are showing, as always.

"Whatever," she echoes back.

The upstairs door closed and footsteps ran away from the door of the basement.

Hoop was trying to settle the cover over his head again, but his hand knocked the back of a stair. The sound was enough to alert the girl. She whirled around with the umbrella raised over her head, ready to throw or strike.

"JaniceIwon'thurtanyofyou," Hoop whispered before she could scream or run, before she knew who she was seeing — that wet forehead, those two dark eyes, which were vibrating, barely, like a tuning fork, from fear to fatigue to anger to madness. He was wrapped in her old comforter. He looked like an Old Testament prophet.

Hoop saw the next two hours in a second. His mother's agonized image, the lines from her nose to jaw, her overprocessed hair, the carpet of the eleventh floor hallway, flanked by two soldier cops, Echo's thousand pockets and bazooka, the door opening inward, his mother's heavy bottom lip, one hand on the door. And he could read inside her too. She'd think *don't answer* at the knock. She'd think of herself in church, *God give me strength to raise my child in this country.* And in a few months, in the winter, she

---

Looking through one of the back bedroom windows of an unfinished house, Hoop and Duane, girlfriendless, observe a girl outside crossing tread marks of hardened mud.

Duane looks to see if he'd hit that.

Hoop looks to see if he knows her.

would think of his deviance, his big, expensive feet, while riding the bus between jobs, double-socked, in white no-name sneakers, and she would curse the cold cold winters of this country, and remember her government job in Jamaica, then fall asleep with her head on the window in someone else's grease patch.

Tears came when Hoop blinked. "Please," he said.

o o o

Tasha ran back to the door and opened it when she heard Janice's footsteps approaching the top.

"Did you see the killer?"

"Uh uh."

"I just wasn't sure if they checked," said the mother from the kitchen. "Come eat."

"Girl, you look scared," said Tasha.

o o o

Moments later, a guy emerges from the same house, dusting the front of his vest, looking both ways, putting a thumb to a nostril and sniffing tough-man style, then he picks up a slight limp and exits the site.

Hoop wants to hurt him. Duane wants to check out the house they came from. He puts a fist to his mouth and *whoop whoop*s. Starting to limp himself, he walks from the bedroom and says, "That's what I'm talkin' 'bout."

Hoop could no longer hear them, only the zooming sounds of segments changing on the entertainment show. The volume was higher. Janice must have been whispering everything up there, then they'd barricade the basement door, call the cops, then there'd be a loudspeaker and handcuffs and dogs and a helicopter whirring and a camera and *Bad boys, bad boys, whatcha gonna do?*

He started making a deal with God. *Lord, if you, if You, could get me out by some miracle*—How had he known Janice's name? Was that her name? Her name had come so easily to him, though he didn't recall noticing it, unlike the mother's bills on the patio furniture. *God if You, if YOU, could find a way out of this situation for me, then I'll*—Her room, that's where. On the door she had stuck up *Janice's room Keep out!* like a white girl would, Hoop thought, but he had been so distracted by the poster of some glistening, thick-legged, R&B singer, hair blowing like a horse, that he didn't remember the sign.

Then I'll what? Anything you want, Lord Jesus. That's how his mother prayed, every time there was a pause, she would fill up the space with *Lord Jesus*, barely aware that she was saying it.

Hoop made God an offer. But He could refuse. So Hoop started planning his explanations. *It was somebody else's idea. This guy*

Doorbell. There's a security sign on the front glass. That's new.

"Who that could be? Tasha don't open."

"I'm not a baby."

"Tasha I said no."

Tasha opens anyway. Ms. Pearson is flapping her hands dry as she approaches the door.

at school, I heard him talking so I tried it. I wasn't looking for anything, I just wanted to see if I could do it. Play dumb, good. *Or I was curious about how the inside of The Houses looked now that they're finished. There wasn't any car in the driveway. I thought this one hadn't closed yet.* [Didn't you see the shoes and the mat, the furniture?] *Yeah, as soon as I saw all that, the people came and I got scared so I hid.* Better. [What about all the stuff in your bag?] Dang.

The basement door opened again and Janice stepped down to the landing to collect some plastic bags — that's where they kept them, stuffed in a garbage bag, and when she took one more step down from the landing (Hoop could have grabbed her ankle to plead again or just slit her tendon with the boxcutter), she called up with her grappling-hook voice, "I need some air. We should go out."

"So late?"

"It's not late." The plastic bags hissed. "I at least need some air, but I'm not walking around by myself with some crazy in the neighbourhood."

She was at the top of the stairs again, her ankle was out of reach. Light flossed through the crack in the door.

"All right, just now, after Tasha brush she teeth."

"Um," Hoop says. He scratches his nose. He'll have to lie. "I go to Janice's school. She left this behind and I just..."

"Janice!" her mother shouts.

"You don't have to call her. Here, just give it to — "

"Come inside. She coming. Janice!" Ms. Pearson hurries back to the kitchen, slapping her slippers against the tile.

Still Hoop didn't trust her completely. She was evacuating the
house so they'd be safe to call the police and dogs, camera, helicopter, *bad boys, bad boys,* etc.

But then footsteps ran down the upper staircase, Tasha protested wearing a coat when Janice didn't have to, chairs were
cleared from the entrance, and the front door closed loudly. Hoop
waited a few moments in case someone had forgotten her keys
or needed to come back to pee. His heart was accelerating again.
When the upstairs was still, he came out of hiding, willed his sore
knees up the stairs and out the side entrance. He walked to the back
of the house, cut across the unfenced back lawns and came out on
the main road. Not safe enough. He kept his eyes on the intersection, where the buses travelled more frequently. He pulled the
intersection toward him with his eyes because he couldn't run.
He had to walk as slowly as anyone watching would expect him
to in those jeans and ball shoes.

Hoop steps inside. They've installed bolts on the front door and
the one leading to the garage. At the end of the hallway he sees
real furniture. Leather.

Janice comes down the stairs. Tasha walks back to the staircase
and says *ooh* with her back to Hoop.

He holds out a baseball hat, then he takes his MP3 player from
his pocket. "I found it, just now, back by The Houses." He points
a thumb over his shoulder.

He should have left his stash behind, but his prints were all over everything. Not that he had a record. Pay them back. A thank-you note — just to the girl, Janice.

He wanted to go home directly and go to sleep, but he took the knapsack to Duane's place first, in the apartment building near his. He shook out the booty on Duane's bed, lied and said he found it in Phase II of The Houses. Duane photographed everything and put it online. Hoop didn't care for the items either — what, a charger, a small video game, a cheap MP3 player, two brand name baby tees. No laptop, no digital camera.

Only the baby tees didn't sell. Duane and Hoop split the money, unevenly, and spent it on cafeteria lunches, dumping the ones their mothers prepared.

For days, Hoop listened to the news on AM radio, but there was no mention of 23L. Thank God there was worse news. A carjack on the east end, subway evacuations, insurgents overseas. It would be old news after a day anyway, and really nothing worth mentioning was stolen.

It's not mine you best get the hell out of here who do you think you are coming to my mother's house with your broken guilt trying to be all hero acting like you know me you don't know me fool you think you got my back I said you best run before I call the police on your skinny wannabe gangsta self I take you on myself nigga is what Janice would say outside, but not in this house. On this floor.

Hoop had made a deal with God underneath the basement stairs that if He got him out of this one, he'd — it had taken Hoop a while to come up with something sufficiently attractive for God to say *deal* — go to church with his mother again, read the Bible cover to cover, pay back seven times the money. He had specified his end of the deal: to escape wasn't enough, he'd need a guarantee that he would never get caught, specifically that word would never get to his mother. For that, he'd have to throw down more promises. Does the Lord have a price? He'd give up ball. He'd give up balling. He wouldn't ever take a girl to The Houses, wouldn't touch a girl till he was eighteen, till he was married.

I can get you out, the Lord said, but there will always be someone on your back.

You have to guarantee, Lord Jesus.

Then no deal.

Ms. Pearson comes padding back in her slippers. She looks at Janice. She looks at Hoop. Hoop pulls up his pants with one hand and scratches the back of his neck with the other.

"You," she says.

II

ooo

TRIOS

CRIMINAL ACTIVITY

SHALL BE SENTENCED TO IMPRISONMENT FOR LIFE

There's a bomb under his shirt, strapped across his chest. There are two bombs actually: one under his shirt—Miriam hears that one ticking—and another around his waist.

Once he snuck up behind her as she was running to the bus stop and, midstride, her hand swung back too far and knocked something hard.

"My belt." Heath held up his hands as if to the police. "It's not what you're thinking."

She eyed him. What was he doing following so closely?

"Or my phone," he said, then groped himself until he discovered it wasn't on him. "No, it was my buckle. Really. Look."

When he lifted his shirt, she raised her elbow to cover her eyes, ready for the explosion. In the milliseconds before darkness, she glimpsed the bomb, its sticks of red dynamite tied together, its long wick dangling. When she lowered her arm again, Heath's shirt was down and the bus had arrived.

Now, thrown against him in a taxi whipping round a corner, Miriam's ear falls against his chest. She hears the bomb ticking. She has to push against two flattish, square boxes on his chest to right herself.

"One hundred percent Canadian muscle right there," he says. He spreads his arms gallantly across the backseat and points down with his nose. His legs are open. The bomb palpitates through his thin shirt.

"You know what?" Miriam says quickly. "I think I left something behind."

"What?"

"My — what's it called?" She rifles through her purse.

"We can turn back."

"No, it's fine, it's fine. You go ahead," Miriam says, then leans forward to the driver. "Would you let me out here? How much do I owe?"

"Don't worry about it," Heath says.

Miriam opens the door before the taxi has stopped completely.

"Sorry about this, Heath," she says. "I just really need to get my — You know how it is."

When Heath slides to that side of the cab, she thrusts the door at him like a shield, and scurries away in her heels, purse swinging.

A pair of toonies, with their large areolae of the Queen, wink at him from the seat.

The detonation button is on his left side and shaped like a nipple.

The next day, he puts his elbow on top of her cubicle wall. She sees a cord, a bluish one, running up his arm, so faint it seems to be under his skin.

"Did you find whatever it was you forgot last night?"

"Yes." Miriam's eyebrows form a sine wave. "Yes, thanks, I did."

"Because I thought maybe I did something that made you uncomfortable." Heath comes into her space and sits down. The front of his khakis bulge.

"No, no."

"I thought you thought I was referring to my — "

"No! Why would I think something like that?"

"I've only started working out. It was just a little joke. You know that, right?" He bends his head to catch her eye but her gaze is fixed elsewhere.

"Don't — don't be — " Her eyebrows curl again. "You thought you — You didn't offend me."

He follows her eyes. "They're supposed to be wrinkle-resistant, but I should have ironed them."

Heath is about to smooth his pants when fast-thinking Miriam throws him a pad of Post-its.

"Catch."

o o o

"And he just sat there," Miriam later explains. "*I* couldn't leave because it was my office."

"Cubicle," her mother corrects.

o o o

Heath fans through the Post-its. "I've been keeping something from you."

She doesn't answer. The bulge.

He slides closer and takes a deep breath. "We work together, Miriam, by which I mean we spend a lot of time together, at least in this environment, this environment being our respective cubicles, yours over here and mine over there." Heath speaks as if he's approaching a runway. "What I'm getting at is that this environment is only one kind of environment where two people — "

"Heath — "

"Hang on. I'm going somewhere with this."

"I know where you're going. And we shouldn't." Miriam is unusually calm, like a hostage negotiating for her life. "Heath, it's best — *you know* it's best — for us to keep some distance between us."

"Professional space."

"We shouldn't get too close."

He misunderstands, just hangs his head without moving away.

o o o

"Heath got shut down!" his gym buddy announces in the weight room.

"Shut up."

o o o

Heath stays away for a time. Miriam should be relieved, but only finds herself wondering if he's still wearing the bombs. She thinks her initial suspicion about dynamite was wrong. She got the century wrong. He has a biochemical weapon, a tube with a virus he bought in Amsterdam or Thailand.

She tries to time her departures so they don't meet at the bus stop anymore. But one evening, it seems like he's hovering and she has to watch carefully before she can make a break for the elevator. She gets there, but the elevator takes a while to arrive, and by the time she gets inside Heath is running toward her. She presses *close* frantically, but he manages to slide his upper body and silver briefcase between the closing doors.

"Don't worry, I'm okay," he says, rotating his shoulder.

The briefcase lies collapsed on his shoes. It seems bulletproof.

"You like it?" Heath asks, looking down at his briefcase.

"It's better than what you had before."

He speaks to her with mock confidentiality, shooting his eyes around the elevator. "It's where I keep my top secret, classified information." He raps against the case.

When they reach the lobby, he lets her exit first. She is careful not to swing her arms too much.

"You move or something?" Heath says. "You're never on our bus anymore."

"These days I try to go by my mother's place before heading home."

"She all right?"

"Yeah, no, she's — " What's in the briefcase? "She's just working on this, this thing, and she needs me."

"What kind of thing?"

"You know, like gardening. Flowers. Vegetables. Flowers and vegetables. Lot of work. But you know me, clumsy clumsy. Like that day when my hand hit your — "

"It was my belt!" Heath says, parting his jacket. "Look."

"Your bus is coming."

"Why can't you look?" He slides the belt from his waist with a flourish. Exhaust dissipates behind him like a dying mushroom.

"You should go." Miriam takes a few steps back.

"Do you want to share a cab?"

"I'm not going that way tonight."

And because no one bothers to check, no one even suspects, Heath gets on the bus and goes off.

"Is this seat taken?"

"No."

So he takes it. And he takes a different one, next to a different woman, each day, until he finds Shauna.

"Is this seat taken?" The familiar pickup.

"No," she says, smiling into his hook.

o o o

Strangely, Shauna will not remember anything else Cash says during that first meeting in the staff cafeteria. He doesn't say much. But by the time he leaves, he knows her name, her number, her building, the habits of her evenings.

"You've got something near your lip," he says.

She attempts to wipe it off.

"Here, let me get it." He reaches his thumb across the table.

After he has secured the hook, there is a little blood or lipstick at the side of her mouth.

000

In her sleep, she nibbles her lip.

You've got something here let me get it.

000

Little by little. This is how he takes her over. A finger at a time. A hand. The top lip, then the bottom. The mouth. Her hair, then her head.

Cash is generous like no man she has ever known. If she points out something she likes, he wanders back into that aisle when she's at the register or pretends that he forgot something or kisses her and tells her to go wait in the car. Then he presents her with matching key chains, matching cups, matching towels, matching bathrobes, matching pajamas.

"One for you. One for me," he says.

Shauna presses them to her heart and lets her shoulders drop in overwhelmed appreciation.

Then the line changes: "It's something we can share." A used car. A place with a yard. A bed.

000

After the cups, the marmalade, the tea, after the sunsets and the door-yards and the sprinkled streets, after the novels, after the teacups, after the skirts that trail along the floor, Cash starts to feel funny.

"Whipped," his friends explain and make *wuh-choo* noises.

"Mature," Shauna says.

"You've got it backward," they tell him. "Shauna's running the show."

"They're disgusting. Who needs 'em?" she says while cradling his head.

He wakes up late and gets dressed in a hurry, putting on whatever he can find. It's only when he looks in the rearview mirror to back out of the driveway that he realizes he is wearing Shauna's clothes, her coat, her shoes. Her eyes, mascara applied to the lashes, look back at him. A lock of her hair falls into his face.

He has put her on. She fits tight. He stretches himself out inside of her. At red lights, he adjusts her face over his own, adjusts the webs between his fingers. Over railroad tracks and bumpy roads, parts of his new body shudder.

0 0 0

They do things together. They have a daughter. They stop doing things together.

0 0 0

Eventually he outgrows Shauna. He uses her mouth as a neck hole and takes her off like a T-shirt, ripping whatever needs to be ripped to get out.

At first, he gets his daughter on Friday evenings. Then he gets her every other weekend. He has a habit of returning her late, gummy worms drooling from her mouth. The girl likes to pretend she's a walrus while her parents bicker, while her father says, "She's my daughter too. You have her all week, and then you bawl me out for having her an extra hour. One hour! One hour, Shauna!"

"All I'm saying is if you're gonna be late, call. What's so hard in that?"

So he calls one Sunday: "We're going to be late."

"Why?"

There's no reply.

"She has school tomorrow, you realize that. You realize that, right?" Shauna looks at her phone. *Call ended,* it says.

o o o

In an aisle, Cash's daughter grabs a handful of gummy worms and takes them to him.

"Daddy, I want some," she says and dumps the worms into his hand.

"Sure, baby. Go get some for Daddy too." When she runs back down the aisle, he slips them into his pocket. Outside she slips her little hand into his. They're going fishing.

o o o

Shauna waits a day before calling the police. She parks across the street from her daughter's preschool at 12:15, and although she called that morning and knows her daughter is not there, she waits until the last child exits. Then she puts her head on the steering wheel and weeps.

She tells the police that her ex has kept her daughter.

"And you think he's abducted her for good?"

"I know he has her. He *has* her. Like some kind of hostage."

The officer scribbles on his notepad. "And where would he be?"

Shauna stares, open-mouthed, at the officer. Her strength drains away.

The police immediately check all the wrong places: her classroom, the room Cash rents, his friends' rooms.

000

Cash is two and a half hours north with a fish hooked and fighting at the end of his line. (*Now that I've taken her, what can I do?*) His daughter is near their tent, clapping her hands at the seagulls waddling around her. (*Keep her. Let her go.*) She comes running in time to see the fish flop itself to death. He grabs hold of it, forces his weight down on its head and tail.

"You catch a fish," the girl announces.

"Sure did," Cash says, wiggling the hook backward through its mouth. "Hand Daddy his knife."

"A big fish."

It's really not, but he agrees.

"Where's the bait?" she asks.

"Fish ate it."

"The fish ate the fish on the hook?"

"Yup."

"Then we eat the fish?"

"That's right."

"Then who eat us?" She hands him the knife.

He turns the fish on its side and cuts off its head, then scales it, slits its belly to the anus, and guts it. He does this so quickly that it doesn't seem significant.

"Who eats us?" he repeats her question, walking to the water to rinse his hands.

"Yeah."

Suddenly he turns and runs toward her with claws for hands. She squeals. He lifts her off the ground and nips at her shoulder, her ear, her forehead, her cheek. He turns her upside down and kisses her belly, her tucked-in knees, with his teeth.

"I'm going to eat you," he says. "Yes I am, yes I am."

At her age, she does not understand what is possible. One minute she is pounding at him with her little fists and the next her skin is scaling off and the next she is disappearing into something like sleep. And her body is both outside and inside and too small.

o o o

"Let me look at you. Oh, baby, you're sunburned. And what happened to your mouth? Did he hit you? Did Daddy hit you, baby? Give Momma a kiss."

"I didn't hit her. Listen."

"Then how did she get this?"

"I didn't hit her, Shauna. Listen." Cash grabs her arm. "Listen to me. We were just fishing. She missed preschool. *Preschool*, not school. She learned more out there with me than in a year of that glorified babysitter's. Look, it won't happen again. This doesn't have to go back to court."

Shauna jerks her arm away. Cash grabs it again. "Oh that's exactly where it's going. You are a thief—"

"How can I steal my own daughter?"

"and a liar—"

"Explain that to me."

"and if you ever come near us again—let go of me—I will personally see to it that you never father another child. I said take your hands off me."

But he doesn't, he wrestles her backward into a wall, and, to free herself, she hooks him in the neck.

For breakfast, Lainey has an egg fried in mayonnaise because she's broke and alone and forced to be creative with what's left in the fridge. By midmorning she's heaped beside the toilet, eyes rolled back, trying to avoid the crazy woman in the bowl, the woman with the guppy mouth, opening and closing, eating or speaking or drowning. The woman's face is sometimes a tornado. And she makes a sucking noise when she goes away, but then she comes back. *Who are you crazy lady?* the woman says. *Crazy lady.*

"Where are you Lainey, baby?" Preston's voice is roving through the apartment. "Lainey baby."

Lainey wakes up. She must have fallen asleep, she figures, without losing her sense of being conscious.

Preston opens the bathroom door. He is wearing camouflage pants. His nostrils curl in disgust. "What happened to you?"

"What happened to you?" she says back. He didn't come home last night, and whenever she called his phone went to the message service.

"Fix yourself up." He throws a washcloth at her face and walks away. The TV goes on.

It takes Lainey some effort to get to her feet, even with this new anger as fuel. Her body seems ill-designed, her feet too small and narrow to support all the limbs above them.

When she makes it out of the bathroom, Preston is emptying his pockets on the coffee table while a group of sportscasters say *linebacker, defensive line, last season, rushing, statistics, safety.*

"Tell me. Where were you?" she says.

He reaches inside a brown paper bag. "Did you eat? I brought you a muffin."

"Where were you?"

"My mother's."

"Bull."

"You want the muffin or not?"

"Don't come in here with your muffin and your *Lainey baby* and think that'll make everything all right."

He bites into the top and turns up the volume. *Turnovers, interception, incompletes.*

"Where the hell were you all night?" She jabs the back of his head. "Where were you, Preston?"

He smells as stale as his undershirts and the inside of his hat and also as if he had a good time somewhere with smoking, beer-drinking women. She runs back to the bathroom on tiptoe, hand to mouth.

000

"Where're your parents?" her preschool friend asked while they drew pictures of their families.

"They work in China. You can only get there if you dig a big hole." Lainey drew them in because all the other kids did.

"Why are your parents so small?"

"They're far away." No one noticed the white crayon scribbled over them, rippling the edges of their bodies.

0 0 0

Back on the floor of the bathroom, Lainey rehearses lines. "I'm moving out," she will say. "You've driven me out," she will say. "Every day with you makes me sick."

Preston will repeatedly open and close four fingers to his thumb: *talk, talk, talk.*

She rehearses an alternate version. "Get your things and get out." "I bet your parole officer would like to know where you were." Or simply, and with corresponding gestures, "I'm cutting you off. We're done. Finito."

What did Preston say once? *Cut my head off and it'll grow right back? Cut my head off and you cut off your own?* Whatever it was, someone was being decapitated.

0 0 0

By high school, everyone had grown a second head and extra limbs. Couples clicked down the hall like two-headed spiders, weaving around each other delicately. Lainey spent much of her time just off school property in a defunct tennis court reserved for smokers called The Cage. There were two-headed beasts there too.

Preston, keeper of The Cage, broke apart and limped to her. She looked at his dangling arm, his lame leg, at how he stuck out his bottom lip, and felt sorry for him.

She hooked her arm around his neck and dragged him to her house.

In front of the television, he asked, "Where are your parents?"

"They got a divorce."

"I meant now, stupid."

She left the couch and went to the kitchen. "Do you want something to drink?"

"Which one do you live with?"

"Do you have enough smokes for the two of us?" she shouted back.

He surprised her with what was in his pocket.

o o o

She must have fallen asleep again. When she wakes up, she is not sure how much of the day has happened. For instance, was it snowing in the living room? Was Preston licking her coffee table while she made herself a mayonnaise omelet? Did his mother keep calling and leaving messages about muffins?

There was a fight, no? She had planned to say something to him but ended up saying *crackhead junkie*. He was wearing cargo camouflage pants. He started singing, *It's the hard-knock life for us. It's the hard-knock life for us. Steada treated, we get tricked. Steada kisses, we get kicked.* And she ran back into the bathroom and threw up her womb.

It takes Preston hours to feel sorry enough to join Lainey in the bathroom.

o o o

The woman in the toilet bowl is Preston's mother, buttoned to the neck, hair pulled back severely, ears rotated forward like a cat, everything about her paying attention. She has a habit of emphasizing words as if proving a point to an invisible partner beside her.

"A cashier. Isn't that lovely?"

Patronizing, Lainey thinks.

"My son is dating a checkout girl. What do your parents do, dear?"

"They're dead."

"That's not funny," Preston's mother says.

"I'm not joking."

"What a sense of humour my son's girlfriend has." His mother adjusts her earring. "Wishing her parents dead."

"Nobody's wishing."

"Tell me," Preston's mother says with the feigned nonchalance of a TV lawyer, "just how long have they been dead?"

"Always," Lainey says. To the best of her knowledge, they were born dead. She was born when they were already dead.

o o o

It takes Preston hours to feel sorry enough to approach Lainey. *Post-game analysis, in-depth coverage, video highlights.* She is sitting on the rim of the bathtub, head in her hands, knees together, feet apart. He sits next to her and puts his head on her shoulder. When they stand up, they are attached, and she is sorry. She's not sure for what exactly, just sorry for everything, sorry that things happen.

o o o

Sirens. Footsteps up the stairs. A fist against the door. Men's voices. The landlord is out there too, sorting through her keys.

Lainey huddles with Preston in the bathtub behind the green shower curtain, mostly because she happens to be close by. She would just as soon open the door.

In his pockets, the police find what they're looking for. She hears them ripping his head from her shoulder before she feels it. Apart from that, they don't want any part of her at all.

She gets herself down the stairs to watch them duck Preston's head into the police cruiser. Her reflection stares back from the back window, and behind it, his face. He frowns at her suspiciously, as if contemplating a strange animal. Then he mouths something. She can only tap the glass before the car rolls away.

To keep her balance on her way up to the apartment, she must hold on to the railing, a long cord with no end.

0 0 0

With Preston gone, Lainey saves enough money to buy a ring, which she wears on her left hand. If people ask, she will say, "I got married over the summer."

And they will say, "Really, and you didn't invite us?"

And she will say, "It was private."

And they will say, "Where is he? What's he doing these days? Why don't we ever see him?"

And she will say, "China. Do you want something to drink? You have any smokes?"

Eventually everyone will stop asking. Eventually everyone will leave her alone.

STATISTICS

60% OF BLACK CHILDREN GROW UP WITHOUT A FATHER

I find every other thing to think about except that. It's an American statistic anyway. And I am not — people can't be statistics. Statistics are for a man with an overbite, a steno pad, and pants that could be let down at the hem an inch. Don't think about them. Don't think about my father, who is definitely not a statistic, and what will be a long, shifty-eyed conversation in an Indian restaurant about the seventeen plus years since we last saw each other because there are other things to think about such as not looking like a mama's boy, which is how he must remember me, small-boned, sickly, like my pants could be let down at the hem an inch. Wear pants that fit, sissy.

I've spent the morning slightly disoriented because, let's say, it's my first time back in Canada since my mother bought this new house, and I am still not used to it. As I'm stepping into pants with a 34" inseam, before driving to my mother's school where I'll drop off her car and take the bus the rest of the way into Toronto, something breaks in the kitchen. I'm upstairs so I don't actually see it fall, whatever it is. I hear it shatter like two cymbals clanging together. Coming down the stairs I tally all possible breakable objects. (My heart.) Maybe a plate in the drain tray tipped backward, or maybe the ceramic bowl for cherries and chennette, when they're in season and available at the West Indian store, fell from the counter, where I obviously must have mislaid it while rushing around trying to make it to the restaurant on time (heartbreak), but the crashing sound was higher and more expensive than that, not just the *krrrr* of the cherry bowl, but more of a *khhhh*. I also think, Someone has broken in, smashed the window, and is now wriggling over the sink to the floor. I think, God forgive me of all my sins, just in case there's a man in the kitchen—almost certainly a man, wearing a bandana and oversized clothes. I could take him. I took a few years of karate in a free after-school program, because my father thought— Don't think about him.

In the doorway to the kitchen I see what fell. The lightshade. It was a white globe that came with the house, an imitation sun. The splatter is tremendous, like blood after a gunshot at close range. There are large white pieces directly under the bulb, and the further from the centre, the smaller the pieces become until there are only particles on the family room hardwood and the dining room broadloom. Finally, here's something worth thinking about. How fast does something have to fall to shatter like that? If I duplicated all the conditions, held a new lightshade over my head and let go, how many tries would it take before the same pattern was duplicated? (What is the economic pattern of father-less households?) I mean, does shattering follow the snowflake principle? (What does emotional shatter look like neurologically?) What if you rotated the arrangement ninety degrees, took gravity out of the equation but kept the same rate of acceleration, adjusted the distance and thickness of a windshield, and shot a real person through it, a black man, say, with a nose and everything, not just a crash test dummy, would the exploding glass hit a wall in the same pattern?

Yes, think about the physics. Even a simple, slack-lipped *how in the world?* is better than thinking about—

It's inexplicable. Sixty percent of black children grow up without, without a. If the lightshade didn't fall because of my ineptitude (how many insurance underwriters does it take to screw in a light bulb?) then it must have fallen because I was stomping upstairs, trying to rush out so I could catch the Jane St. bus at noon (one to screw it in and three to stand back and assess the risk), although TTC buses don't run on any objective schedule that I can discern apart from every ten or fifteen minutes, but they always seem relatively late. Relative. Block. I must have been stomping like the woman in the condo above mine in New Haven, the woman who seems to jump on one part of the floor over my chandelier in the hallway, setting off a sound like metal striking glass or like the reverberation of some doorbells after you ring them. All hours she does this. Sixty percent! I haven't found the courage to confront her, casually of course, because she is blonde, single, thin as a cell phone, an heiress to a family (Family. Block. Block.) business, and because when driving home late, I slow down and look into her windows, if the shades happen to be up, to see if this might be the night that she runs from the bathroom to the bedroom to retrieve a bra. I must have inadvertently picked up stomping from her, because I am not an angry and abandoned statistic who stomps or shoots angry and abandoned statistics in the ghetto.

Although I'm late for lunch with my, with my, with my— why not call him *dad* or *pop* or *pa?* —I decide to sweep up what I can, meaning whatever landed on the tiles and hardwood. Even if I won't be able to explain the falling, I'll have to explain the mess to my mother, who has made it a habit to sweep kitchens twice a day since she was nine years old. A few hurried brushes at the carpet just make the pieces pop up and settle back into the fibres instead of popping forward into the dustpan, so I'll have to sweep the same spot several times to dislodge all the fragments, and I don't have enough time to do that because there's a man in an Indian restaurant waiting to see if my pants fit.

Self-sabotage. That's what's going on here. I'm already half an hour behind schedule and I'm sweeping up glass, barefoot, hoping to injure myself, to cut either my foot or my hand deep enough to draw blood, to drive myself to Emergency and tell my father later, by phone, that I got hurt on the way to Bombay Delight, that's why I didn't show up. And then when he finds out that it was only a piece of glass the size of a paperclip he'll think that I'm lacking courage, thin-skinned, a mama's boy, a sissy, no child of his.

I leave the pieces in the dustpan to show my mother I made a good effort to clean up, and I leave the dustpan in the middle of the kitchen floor. It looks as if I'm coming right back, perhaps after locating the appropriate vacuum attachment. In fact, I'm in the car, accelerating irresponsibly out of the suburbs, through various school zones, without my seat belt, hoping to catch the attention of a cop, but a lenient one who would delay me twenty, twenty-five minutes then give me a warning, while a man is probably already seated in Bombay Delight, drinking water, checking the time on a practical, water-resistant digital watch.

At a red light, I find a bank deposit envelope in the pocket of the car door and write my mother a note: *The lightshade in the kitchen broke. I don't know how. Be careful where you walk. I'll tell you how everything went later.* No *love.* No name.

120   Ian Williams / STATISTICS

It rains and rains and rains later that day.

[   ]

After eating chicken roti with a knife and fork at the Indian restaurant, and walking around in the rain looking into storefronts to see
the spectacle of myself, a soggy khaki mess, I call my mother to see
if she would fetch me from the bus terminal. I feel like I'm twelve
doing this. In the car, she just has to begin a sentence about the
broken shade and I launch into a spiritless explanation and defense.
I was late. I don't know how. I wasn't even in the room.

"It's an omen," she tells me. The word is kohl-coloured and
swollen like the sky. I think of dead birds. I think of the bare coiled
bulb hanging from the kitchen sky. *What does it mean? What does
it mean?*

"Someone's going to die?" I say.

"Something go happen." She is driving more slowly than usual.
"You remember when your father was leaving Trinidad. Maybe
you was too small to remember."

"I remember," I say before I can be sure what's she's talking
about.

"All the bulbs in the house blew. And I wanted to know how all
the bulbs in the house could blow like that — at the same time. You
remember?"

I can't be sure whether I'm remembering or imagining. "Vaguely."
"That was an omen. Because after" and she doesn't need to finish.
Everybody knows what happened after.

o o o

43% OF FIRST MARRIAGES END IN DIVORCE OR SEPARATION WITHIN FIFTEEN YEARS

One minute we were eating roti with our hands in the dark. Then part of his finger was bleeding. Then people were saying get over it.

But your father's finger didn't bleed a little viscous bubble as from the prick of a blood sugar test or from a deeply cut fingernail. The blood didn't come from his fingertip. It didn't come from the lines in his knuckle either, like when it gets too cold and your skin dries until it bleeds. That's how your skin weeps in this country, not with sweat but blood. One minute we were eating roti in the dark. The next minute his finger was bleeding in the kitchen. Then *boom* people were saying, Ah quit your whining and get over it.

We were talking about mango trees. We had just bought our first townhouse. It was narrow and made of concrete. Sometime between paying the last of the down payment and moving in, the house had been visited, probably checked out for a later robbery. There were dusty footprints. We couldn't afford to change the locks so soon because of the down payment, because we had borrowed money from everybody and couldn't ask for more, but we never said those reasons aloud. Your father said something like, No one would dare break into the house now that it's occupied. He'd defend it with cutlass and machete. *Dare, cutlass,* and *machete* are his words. *It* also; he didn't say he'd defend *me*. We had stolen two light bulbs from where we lived. One for the kitchen, one for the bedroom. But we were so hungry we didn't screw them in, just sat ourselves at the bottom of the stairs, I between his legs, and ate roti straight from the foil with our hands in the dark. Part of his finger bled later. People said, Why she can't get over it?

Your father wanted a mango tree. I wanted a cherry tree. There was no reason we couldn't have both, but the night we were eating roti, we went on like we had to choose one. To pass the time. We liked fighting on low heat now and then. To pass the time. The soil was good although some of our neighbours would call it clay, call the neighbourhood a shantytown, sing calypsoes against the government. But the National Housing Authority had done us no serious wrong. We practiced our story, not because it was untrue and needed to be synchronized, but because it was what people did back then—practiced for interviews, dressed up for them, put on their best British manners, brought their birth certificates and proof of their O-levels and A-levels, and spoke in whispers when the civil servant left the room. The housing officer took one look at us and started writing. There are stories about interviews being determined from when you walked in the room; the officer would leave a handkerchief or some money on the floor and whoever picked it up would get the house. At the end he said we'd hear from him in three months, meaning four in Trinidad time, four and a half on the calendar, so long that we thought our application had been denied. We were low on the priority scale, he said. It would be three years before we got a house. Longer than our engagement. Your father wanted a mango tree. I wanted a cherry tree. He wanted a boy. I wanted a girl. We got everything we wanted.

We ate roti on steps in the dark. Your father's finger bled. People said, Just get over it.

We left the house before the mango tree could bear. We ate the cherries though. Birds ate them. We sent you and your sisters out in flip-flops through long grass and picker bush to collect your shirts full. The mango tree, people said, would take five years to bear. We never ate from that tree. It sounds Biblical. Expelled from our land, never to eat from the tree we planted. We didn't think that would happen when we were young—as young as you are now—and eating curry chicken roti. Your father with a cut finger. People said it would take five years. Get over it.

Someone else is eating from that tree, thinking that it came with the house, that no one planted it. We left it. Everybody had to leave something. You left your train with the face painted on the front, your least favorite G.I. Joes. You might remember that. We bought you new shoes. Your father made a big deal over teaching you and your sisters the difference between *emigrate*, to leave one country or region to settle in another, and *immigrate*, to come to a country of which one is not a native, usually for permanent residence. We became permanent residents; that's actually what the visa said. Why proper usage became so important to you father, I don't know. But he was insistent on everyone saying *emigrate from Trinidad* and *immigrate to Canada*. One presumed you were leaving, the other coming. We lived between *em* and *im* for a year. You and sisters drew pictures and I mailed them with my letters to your father. He wouldn't have cared for the pictures if everyone were together back home, but later we found he had saved them all in the pocket of his briefcase, folded preciously into six, not three like business letters. I left behind my sewing machine, the curtains, the wares, the trees, the NHA house, the blown bulbs. Everything I shipped fit in a corner of the dining room. What I couldn't ship,

I sold. What I couldn't sell, I gave away. What I couldn't give away, I threw away. What I couldn't throw away, I left. The mango tree. Never being able to see how it turned out. Wanting to see a child you gave up now that he's grown. Would the tree be good for chutney or chow or Sunday mornings, good enough to give away, for no-good boys to steal from? With our hands, we ate roti in the dark. Your father cut his finger. People tell me get over it.

Back home/this country. Emigrate/immigrate. Black/white. Everything in relation to a slash. My blackness in opposition to the white — not blue — sky, the white earth, the white air. The people talking up in their nasal cavities. What's not white is transparent — more the colour of ice than water. There is no place to buy roti, far more to buy buss-up-shot. And there is no translation from English to English: it's like roti but not roti, it is exactly what I said it is, a shirt busted up. Your father and I flexed. He wore layers instead of shorts. We shouted our accents at each other in a rented apartment. Fighting someone you love is the best comfort in a country where everyone smiles. We quarrelled to remind ourselves where we came from, long, complex, brutal, strained arguments. What a mirror would be if you could fold it like a letter. Some months we couldn't afford electricity. There was a reconnection fee on top of the unpaid balance. We ate roti in the dark. He cut his finger on a can. To this day, people say, It's over. Get over it.

We were fighting, high heat. I was making supper for you and your sisters. He tried to take the tin because of something I said. Something about money. It might have been, You could provide for anybody? You cyah even mind your own children. And he might have said, Don't eat my food then, and tried to take the tin of sardines. But I held on. He held on. Emigrate your skin from this marriage, I said. He held on. He said, Anybody want you here? I held on. Emigrate from me, nah. We both held on to the tin of sardines, trying to peel the lid back. The frying pan was already on the fire, empty, starting to burn itself. You were there. I ripped the top back. It cut straight down his ring finger, from the corner where the nail breaks with the flesh down almost to the base of the finger, and the skin hung like a banana peel. One minute you're eating roti with your fingers in the dark. Then you nearly cut your husband's finger off with a tin of sardines. And people expect you to get over it.

There was blood in the tin. We had to throw the sardines out. I turned my back to your father, found something to do in the sink, kept frowning, said, Take that, steeled myself, because I thought he might hit me, although he never had. We had stomped, ran at each other, pushed the other around with our shoulders, but never hand to face, hand to head, to arm, to back, to eye, to thigh. Your father drove himself to the hospital, calling you and your sisters to give him a plastic bag so he could wrap the finger and not dirty the car's upholstery. With one hand, he put on his shoes, his coat. He must have driven to Emergency with one hand. From the kitchen to the door, the red drops remained. They were scalloped around the circumference. Each drop of blood nearly identical in size, evenly spaced between the sink and the door. When he came back I couldn't say sorry. I was watching TV. You and your sisters were silent. Your father took off his coat with one hand. His ring finger was bandaged in white gauze. He told you he had six stitches. I turned off the TV. I went to the bedroom. I slept on my side. One minute you're eating roti in the dark. The next you're cutting your husband with a sardine tin. People say, Get over him.

It happened a long time ago, people say. Your children made it out of that area, then out of public housing. Your husband has moved on to another country, another woman. You're stuck, you with your Jheri curl, with your old old story of mango and cherry trees. You with your paid-off car and steady job, your fixed-rate mortgage, your digital thermostat, your son in New Haven, your twin girls married, your clean floors and nine-foot ceilings. One minute, you're eating roti with your hands in the dark. Then your husband gets cut. And people say,

o o o

DIVORCE RATES ARE HIGHEST DURING THE FOURTH YEAR OF MARRIAGE

What I should be — what I am thinking about is the road. I am also thinking about the splatter of rain on the windshield and the trails on the passenger-side window that look like worms crawling backward and diagonally to the rubber weather strip. This is because of the combination of gravity and vehicular velocity. It's also safe to think about changing out of these wet clothes, especially the pants which are soaked through at the hem because they were too long in the first place and I never should have worn them.

My mother is driving at the speed of thought. Slow, but not alert. She is still worrying, I know, about the lightshade. What will happen? What does it mean that a lightshade fell on its own from the kitchen ceiling? Why must the omen come from the ceiling? Why would God intervene so? Look up, for your redemption draweth nigh.

"You're in the wrong lane," I say.

"I'm not."

"You're driving too slow to be in this lane."

"I'm turning."

"Then put your signal on."

"No one's behind me."

"It's the principle. And someone's behind you."

"In the other lane."

"Where you should be."

This is exactly the kind of driving that's becoming more common with her as she gets older. And it's a suburban thing, casual and self-absorbed. When we, all five of us in a Toyota with our Ontario license plate, used to drive down to Florida to visit my father's relatives, we were always impressed by how orderly the Americans drove on their interstates. There were only two lanes in each direction, for the most part, but there was rarely any traffic unless the interstate ran through a city because the Americans would drive in the right lane, pass on the left, then merge, using their signals, back into the right. The dance of it

"What happened with your father?"

"I'll tell you later. Concentrate on the road."

was so courteous and professional unlike this suburban sense of entitlement to every lane whether driving through the cramped historic downtowns or the six-lane divided parkways. My father would drive most of those trips. He would stop every four hours so we could take a break, and if it got dark, he'd pull into a motel, reach into his back pocket for his wallet, and lay down a credit card on the counter and be called *Sir*.

Headlights scream forward. Seatbelts lock. My mother's right arm shoots in front of me to keep me from flying through the windshield. As if she could. A crunch from the back. The driver's side airbag detonates. Then *phooph*.

Our senses dilate.

For the first time, I notice that there is a plaza outside and a pet store and a dollar store and streetlights and rain not just on the passenger window but everywhere outside and sidewalks and storm drains and a couple of teenagers with their hands balled up in the front of their sweatshirts and the *phoop*hing of other cars passing. Where was the world all this time? It blooms so suddenly, blood from a wound.

I see my mother more clearly than I have in years. From behind the leak of the airbag she looks like she's been removed from cellophane. She turns off the engine and says nothing. She is not blinking enough, just staring ahead at the deflated airbag, then at the traffic light which has recently turned red. I don't need to ask if she's okay.

"Are you okay?" The woman who has rammed into our car taps on the driver's window. She winds her hand in a small circle meaning roll down the window. We can read her lips. "Are you okay?"

I step out to assess the damage.

"Are you hurt? Is she okay?"

I walk to the back of our vehicle.

"I thought she was going to turn before the light went red."

The left tail light is broken. Flecks of red glass lie on the asphalt.

"But then she braked."

The pattern is different from the broken lightshade earlier today. This one is more like a spiderweb if you filled in the negative space with red glass and coloured in the silk with a black marker.

"It's my first accident. The rain. I've never hit anybody before."

Or like a digital photo of spilled sugar if you zoomed in.

"Are you her husband?"

"I'm her son," I say.

"Oh."

Does she want to hear about my father? Because I could tell her about seventeen plus years and showing up late at Bombay Delight if she wants to hear, not now but over lunch on an outdoor patio after I get her number and settle this collision business and transform our accidental meeting into a romance destined to happen, with the suave style of a man who has a black book and a scent associated with him.

In the rain, the woman's eyes are bleeding black, beneath her glasses which are speckled with rain, either from the effect of rain or tears on her mascaraed lashes. This is nothing to cry about, I should tell her, if she is in fact crying. Neither my mother nor I sympathize with criers. So quit your cryin'. Wouldn't that make me sound like a man? A little roughness. A mouth like chapped hands. Her hair is matting into fine dreadlocks and dripping on the shoulders of her silky-looking blouse. In another situation, say if I were entering an elevator and came across her, I would find her fairly attractive. In another situation, say if we both met at the office stock cupboard in New Haven to refill our cache of binder clips, I would find her well-spoken, but perhaps not completely genuine, as she asks about my weekend. Polite rather than honest. In another situation, say turning off the ensuite light and stomping to bed, I would find her irritating, touchy, chatty, thin-skinned and glass-spined.

She could be the first woman I marry and divorce. From start to finish, give it four and a half years. No children.

"Is everyone okay?" she says.

Why does she keep asking that? Her concern is not genuine. She is only seeing a potential lawsuit or a fraction of her pay being deducted every month as part of a settlement to take care of the ongoing medical bills of the woman in the car.

"Are *you* okay?" I ask her.

"Just frazzled. It's my first accident."

"You said that."

"How about your mother?"

"I don't know."

"Miss, are you okay," the woman calls out. She walks back to the driver's window.

No answer.

"Does she need to go to the hospital?"

"Give us a minute," I say. "Why don't you get out of the rain for a while?"

The woman goes back to her car, looking over her shoulder at me or the damage, then she pulls out her cell phone.

"She wants to know if you're okay," I say to my mother from the passenger seat.

"That isn't her concern right now."

"It's the most important thing right now."

"You think she care whether I okay?"

"She asked."

"She just don't want to get sued."

The accusation, aloud, is so mean-spirited that I feel the need to defend the woman, although I thought the same thing just now, and thought it so forcefully that I felt I *knew* her concern for my mother was only concern for herself. But it's not something one says. If I were to defend her, as I am in my mind, while at the same time I've already damned her for her silken, polite mock concern, I would tell my mother that she was driving at the speed of thought or, in physical terms, driving a lazy suburban stroll, locked up as she was in some reverie that was only being half communicated to me, that she was driving as if she trusted the car to get us from the bus terminal to our home on a kidney-shaped street, which is how Monarch Crescent would appear from an airplane overhead, and it's because she was driving, ambling, idling forward without any sense of agency in moving the vehicle toward our spot on the kidney bean that we were struck from the back. In effect, we deserved to be hit.

But this woman whom I will possibly divorce in four and a half years is not worth defense. When I look over my shoulder, I see her still talking on her cell, shading her mouth. She is being advised.

"This is the omen," my mother says.

What she means — I know because she and I tend to think alike in crises — is I never should have gone gallivanting through Toronto, in her words, *You shouldna go nowhere*, when God sent such a logical sign this morning that there would be danger involving crashing and glass, and now my wanton disregard for the omen results in endangering not just my own safety but hers. And for what?

"What happened with your father?"

"You realize we're in an accident?" I say. "I'll tell you when we—"

"Tell me now." My mother looks in the rearview mirror as if what happened at Bombay Delight is in view. Over my shoulder, the woman is still on her cell phone being advised.

"I didn't see him."

"I tell you so. You feel I don't know your father."

"I was late. He might have shown up. I was the one who was late. Not him."

She doesn't push. "We shouldn't be on the road at this hour. The lightshade," she says it finally.

If the accident did not happen, the lightshade would still hang over us. Something else would happen and we would say, *the lightshade! the lightshade!* But I don't argue.

Instead, I walk to the woman's car. Silver Kia Magentis, approximately four years old, vanity license plate, minor damage to the left headlight and bumper. In a glance.

She ends her phone call and winds down her window. She blurts out, "I don't want to get the insurance companies involved."

"I work in insurance." Not in the department she thinks, but no need for her to know that.

"It's nothing personal," she says. Rain drums on the roof of her car.

I don't say anything. She'll have to do better than that.

"I'll take care of fixing your car privately. I know a mechanic. He's really good."

Better.

"You'll see. He'll get everything done to your satisfaction."

Not to our satisfaction. We cannot be satisfied.

"What's your number? Let me call you, then you'll have mine."

In a moment my phone rings. Her name is Candace Guardi. I could call her *Candy, Candy Guardi,* over lunch at an Indian restaurant somewhere in Toronto, then fly her to New Haven and tell the men at work, with my arm around her waist, It's *Guardi,* like *LaGuardia,* at least until she hyphenates it for the middle part of the four-and-a-half years we spend together.

"We'll talk in the morning," Candy Guardi says. "I actually should have been somewhere a long time ago."

You too? Nobody's going anywhere.

JOINT

WHILE

At the airport, the world blows around them. Passengers criss-cross, trench coats billow, suitcase handles click, wheels roar, a voice crackles overhead. Because they've stood like this for so long, facing each other and holding hands, they seem to be the only still points in the blur.

Scott wants to reach into his pocket and pull out something worth giving, something like a chickadee or a small bamboo plant, but he has only his keys, his wallet, a loose mint.

"Last chance," he says. "I'll come if you pay."

"Really? You'd trek across Europe at my expense. For me?"

"For you, I'd stand in front of a million splatter paintings. I'd sport a beret and a turtleneck and prance around Paris with a baguette under my arm." He's geeking out, anything to detain her. "You have to call me every day, twice a day. And I don't want to hear about any *huh-huh* business when you're there or I'll have to fly over and whop some — "

"Down, boy." Molly says. She tries to look ready for a kiss.

"Sorry," Scott says.

Their heads move toward each other, but their bodies don't, and their glasses bump when they kiss, so Scott has to readjust his partway through, which means he can't hook Molly close to him. He wants a redo. He watched clips of *From Here to Eternity*, damn it, where Burt Lancaster and Deborah Kerr are kissing on the beach among the crashing waves. Molly should pull away and say, *Nobody ever kissed me the way you do.*

Instead she says, "And, hey, thanks for the ride." Then she walks through the stanchions toward the gate entrance.

"Molly!" Scott calls her back. He shuffles through his wallet for something to give her. "Take this."

His student card. Panic face.

o o o

The first thing Molly realizes is that she, like a good Canadian, is not interesting to anyone. The Parisians were not expecting her and made no preparations for her arrival. So she spends most of her time walking up and down the streets with her red daypack, snapping pictures of palatial facades, cathedrals, and, yes, the genitals of naked sculptures.

She will realize later that she is in very few of these photo-

Sitting on the hardwood floor, steak fries in the oven, Scott watches a hockey game in the dark. During the commercials he flicks over to figure skating, the only sport Molly would condescend to watch. Pairs dancing. The men toss back their hair, stick their butts out. Commentators mispronounce *six*. He misreads *PAIRS* for *PARIS*.

He flicks back.

Something comes over him when Montreal scores, and

graphs, and that Paris is mostly buildings, pigeons, and sky.

worse, when they celebrate, their sweaty heads filling up the screen.

000

Molly finds an outdoor café, and orders in the travel-guide French she knows. She sits outside at the red checkered cloth only because she wants to tell her friends that she did. But she is alone — no one will ever know that — sunglasses on, sipping the froth off a cappuccino.

Paris, he thinks. *Of all places I don't believe in.*

000

"Pourriez-vous prendre une photographie de moi, s'il vous plaît?" she asks a French man whose chest hair tumbles over his shirt.

"Pourriez?" He raises one eyebrow at the word but accepts the camera and takes the photo. "And one more avec moi, cherie."

Before she can protest, modestly, he wraps himself around her waist, and holds the camera at arm's length. Then

Toronto lost because he was not cheering, Scott decides, so he resolves not to watch any more hockey games alone. These are the playoffs. Serious stuff. His buddy, long neglected since Molly, comes over, as Scott knew he would.

"The S-man!" Henry shouts when Scott opens the door. He is wearing a hockey jersey, cap, and giant blue finger.

"You got on the subway looking like that?" Scott asks.

everything speeds up. The audio track of voice is so high the next time he speaks, she can hardly understand him. Her feet stumble behind his as he pulls her along into trains, ritzy lobbies, the Louvre, Pompidou, boutiques. He orders her to stand, turn around, compliments the cut of her calf in this or that dress. He puts Nutella crepes in her hand. The sun bounces up and down.

Why the rush? she wonders. He's unemployed, no doubt, to have all this time.

"Dude."

Chips tonight, not french fries, and a two-litre bottle of ginger ale, which disappoints Henry. But he is still able to do magic: pound his chest twice and belch.

And he is still happy to be with his old friend. He charms Scott back to manhood with wedgies, headlocks, and noogies, and once by digging a spitty finger into Scott's ear. Then they wrestle around, flop on their backs and look at the ceiling, Hockey Night music blaring.

Phone.

o o o

"Scott?"

"Hang on, I can't hear you. Henry, turn that down. It's Molly."

"What are you doing?"

"Watching hockey. Are you all right? Do you need anything?" He takes the phone to the other room and closes the door. Now he can hear someone squeaking French in the background. "Who's that?"

"Mon ami."

"A guy?"

"Scott!" she protests archly. "I can't stay long. I just called to say *au revoir.*"

"Are you leaving?"

"Yes."

"Me or Paris?"

"Paris." She laughs.

"Alone?"

"No." She pauses just long enough to worry him. "With your card."

More mumbling.

"I'll call you from Spain." She doesn't even wait for an answer before hanging up.

"Tell her I say *bonjour*," Henry shouts from the other room.

0 0 0

alone.

"You must come back," the Frenchman says in his inflected English.

"I'll try."

He asks to take a last photograph of her, and, flattered, she gives him the camera. He steps back into the crowd with the camera at his side. The next time he speaks, his voice is at a normal pitch again.

"You must come back."

0 0 0

Henry spends the night. He and
Scott fall asleep with pillows
—goalie pads—belted around
their shins.

0 0 0

On the train, Molly counts
her Euros. She has far less than
she expected, but she spent
a lot, always for two. There's
not enough to return to Paris,
unless she cuts Barcelona and
maybe Florence next week. She
checks the other compartments.
But, there's a credit card, she
forgot about that, and behind
it, Scott's panic face worrying
about *huh-huh*. She forgot
about that too.

THEN

School of

Engineering.

The recipients

of the Doctor

of Philosophy

Degree in

Aeronautics and

Astronautics are:

James Chan

Shu-Min Chow

Sean Davidson

Gloria attends her MIT Commencement
alone. Her father's back in Nebraska greying,
on dialysis three times a week, skeptical of
airplanes. Mother's dead.

The ceremony's outside in Killian Court
over grass that was cordoned off and soaked
for weeks. Gloria feels responsible for the pace
of the procession, as if she were clogging up
the line with her presence. No one is there for
her with an air horn and a *Yeah Gloria!* and
an *Oohoo*.

It's humid. The black gown doesn't help.
And she's sick of everyone's enthusiasm. The
girl on her left rests her hand on Gloria's folded
arm, and says, *Don't you feel like a celebrity?*
and before Gloria can say *I guess* and ask a

Luis Garcia

Morgan Gilmour

Samad Hashmi

Nathan Hunter

Robert Lam

Dmitri Lipnik

Anthony Loh

favour, the girl is chair-hugging someone behind her.

Gloria's here out of duty. Not go to her own graduation? It would be out of character. Extended family members back home are waiting to foist the photographs on their kids for motivation.

A guy is taking his sweet time across the stage. Basking. *Hurry up already*, she thinks at him. *When's my name going to come up?*

Xiaofang Ma, Garth Maki, Caleb Mancini, Magnus Narula, Brandon Ngo, Sherwin Olton, Ana Petrova,

Neil Silver-Soler

Welham Stephen

Nelson Trella Scott

Wong Zhi Yang.

Ladies and

gentlemen,

we kindly ask

that you hold

your applause

until all the

graduates have been

named.

Then a man shouts, *We love you Mommy*, jumping and jiggling a baby like he's at the World Cup.

Gloria's family, her father, is not the cheering type. He might trudge closer to the stage for a photo and try not to cut off her head or stick his thumb over the chancellor. The event feels like a bad recording already, and she will remember the wavy humidity, the robes, a voice calling out names, but not the names themselves, as if she experienced the ceremony without her glasses on and with water in her ears.

Gloria glances at the girl on her left, who doesn't know she's been designated to take Gloria's stage-crossing photograph.

We love you Mommy! Please. The kid must be dying out here.

Thank you for your co-operation. The recipients of the Master

of Science Degree in Biological Engineering are: Nathaniel Cooney,

Robson Glassford, David McIntyre, Elizabeth Osmond

Aaron Sacco	Get your period. Then what? Start high
Franciszek Ksa-	school. Then what? Get a boyfriend. Then
	what? First kiss. Then what? You know.
Ksawery Tr-	Then what? Get your license. Then what?
	Prom. Then what? College. Then what?
Trzes- Trzeszcz-	Grad school. Then what? Get a job.
Trzeszczkowski.	

Excuse me, Franciszek Ksawery Trzeszczkowski.

The recipients	"What an awful name," the girl next to
	Gloria says.
of the Doctor of	"Sounds Polish."
Philosophy Degree	"Shoot him now. Trzzezzezzkowski!"
	Then she changes the subject after Gloria
in Biological	shrugs. "Which job did you take?"
Engineering are:	That's how to ask the question at MIT,
	because everyone finds work.
Kevin Austin	"At UNO."
Donna Beacon	Blank.
	"University of Nebraska, Omaha."
Sohan Brar Adrian	"Nebraska?" Eyebrows. Involuntarily.
Costigan Ronald	"I actually want to be there."
	Disbelief.
DeVito Melinda Fan	"I'm from there."
Katrina Goh	"Oh, then it's okay. How'd you end up
	here then?"
Louis Gomez	*Please, please call my name.*

Mohamed Habib, Thomas Lee, MaryAnn Lee, Ruby Leung,

Xin Liang, Jamie Lyons, Franklin Mann, Carlos Martinuzzi,

Hye-Jin Min

Phoenix Nemy

David Nicholson

George Palazzo

Bradley Purcell

Matthew Rivard

Bharat Sahir

Mitchell Shields

Hyung-Jeong Shin

Ruth Shiner

Ben Tulloch

Lok Chee Wu

Byung-Hee Yoo

The recipients

of the Master of

So how does a girl from the Midwest end up in Chemical Engineering at MIT? Folks are always surprised. She applied. Her grades were good. Midwest had nothing to do with it. Unless MIT had quotas to fill. She did

"Would you take a photo of me when I cross?"

"Sure."

as she was told. There was never a reason to miss a question on an exam if you're only being tested on what you should know. If the book said do this to get that, invariably it worked. Textbooks and Bibles don't lie.

And part of it too is after almost killing her mother in childbirth, doing enough damage to close her womb, she had better *yes miss* to shutting off the TV and *yes sir* to repairing the pickets on the porch. No questions asked. She is forevermore and Amen both son and daughter. Make money and make babies.

Engineering Degree in Biomedical Engineering are:

Paul Danson, Troy Liu, Heather McMullen, Daniel Orr, Markos

Panagiotakakos

The recipients of the

Now what? Buy a car. Then what? Get married. Then what? Buy a house. Then what? Have a kid. Then what? Have

Master of Science Degree in Chemical Engineering are:

Jacob Connelly

another. Then what? You're done. Then what? That's it. Then what? No more. Then what? Stop it. Then what? Dialysis. Then what? You die. Then what? You burn. Then what? Good Lord. Then what? *Call my name.* Then what? Then what? Then what? Then what?

Stefan Rubin, Benjamin Tai, Alan Yeh. The recipients of the Doctor of Philosophy Degree in Chemical Engineering are:

Daniel Barth

Kevin Cho

Paulina Dunn

Natalie Franco

Tanya Gilbert

Ali Hussain

Nancy Kang

Mohan Khan

Dong Hyun Kim

Vijay Kumar

Moon Kwon

Xiang Li

Regis Lorenzatti

Winnie Luo

Bart Nathan

Gloria could have cut back to two meals a day for the ticket, got a wheelchair with an orange flag at Logan airport, drank water two days for a taxi, translated the tunnels from Logan, the towers out the window, fixed him a little supper out of her handbag, cheese on crackers, taken his elbow — *don't pull me* — walked behind him slowly — *don't follow me* — plinked his dentures in a glass with a capful of vinegar, pulled the sheet under his armpits, hummed softly so the neighbours couldn't hear, so softly he'd swear he was remembering, spread her bed on the floor, stayed awake until he was breathing steadily, then snoring, then coughing and sputtering up phlegm in the morning, watched him parachute forward to the bathroom, pushed his arm through his one dress shirt, *Honestly Papo how could you let this old man get you*, brushed his horseshoe, insisted he take a hat for the sun, knotted his tie, spaced the back of his

Ka Ho Ng

Frederick Oh

Peter Oliveira

Seung-il Park

Sarah Popescu

Sunil Rao

Jeremy Raposo

Melissa Sellars

shoe with her finger, bought him senior
fare, exact change, thanked the woman
for giving up her seat, led his hand to the
steel pole, counted him on to the escalator
on three, Papo, one two, lowered him into
a shady aisle seat in Killian close to the
portable toilets, left him with a bottle of
water and her cell phone, showed him how
to answer it, *this button Papo, just press,*
not so long, press and let go — she could
have done all that — for what, then what —
to get her father here for the one second
they said her name

Gloria Serrano

Alicia Usher

Alexander Volpe

Joachim Walsh

Russell Wong

Joseph Yau

No matter how much wheat whistled around
it, he would make out her name, his.

Gloria walks quietly across the stage, gets
her degree, then walks down the ramp to
her seat.

NEXT

31 Sequoia Lane

Went from the semi next door being empty to usually empty but with owners who check on it now and then to definitely occupied by a middle-aged pervert, a man who had nothing better to do than harass Faye. No, she had never seen anybody, but she was certain.

"Maybe it's a ghost."

"Gimme a break." Faye doesn't believe in ghosts.

"Maybe it's a rat. Or Gregor Samsa trying to get out."

"Now you're just mocking me."

33 Sequoia Lane

"Hunchback of Notre Dame. Phantom of the Opera."

There's evidence: knocking from the baseboards, a toilet flushed once, just as she turned on the CBC, her front mat went missing, footprints over her snowy lawn.

Her friend, Denise, wants to laugh. That's before Faye starts fanning back tears.

"I'm telling you," Faye says.

0

So Denise decides to check it out. She parks around the corner and walks down the row of semi-detached houses on Sequoia. She rings the bell of 33 five, six times, then brazenly she fires it. She knocks.

Then, pretending to notice that she's at the wrong house, she walks over to 31. Three locks turn inside, Faye sticks her head out, looks both ways before letting her friend in.

"No one," Denise says. "I rang the bell."

"Of course he's not going to answer the bell."

33 was up for sale, then the sign came down, so it must have been bought.

The sellers never met the buyers. From the beginning, the real estate agent interposed herself between them like an officer blocking a crime scene. For the open house, the sellers were ordered to take down their photos, clear all surfaces, especially the countertops, remove all visible clothing, lock the dog in the garage, and, most importantly, get lost, go for a walk or whatever. Buyers don't want to see the sellers sitting on the couch with a sandwich watching hockey. Their presence knocks 5% off the house.

0

The house didn't sell right away. It was on the market for four months. The sellers became anxious so they dropped the price. The sign came down. The woman next door in 31 moved in. Like that, in that order.

0

"I knocked too."

"Did you walk round back?"

"No." Denise is becoming defensive. "You didn't ask me to."

"You can't go now. Everybody's already seen you. What am I, sending over spies?"

There are no lights on in Faye's house. It's so quiet Denise can hear the occasional car pass on the street.

"Well I'm sorry," Denise says. Faye pats her hand.

"Thanks anyway."

0

Denise can't say anything to Faye, who is beyond reason on the subject, but she has some basic questions. Why would anyone go out of their way to irritate her? Why would this guy hide from the neighbours? If there was someone there, surely someone would have seen him by now (Faye had been living next door for three months). Have you noticed lights on? Maybe he was there, went to London on business. Maybe this guy works early and comes back late.

Looking at 33 from the outside, one can't be sure whether the house is occupied or not.

One can be sure that someone in the neighbourhood is barbecuing, that a woman is jogging behind a stroller, that a bus is lowering itself on the main road for an old man to exit. One can be sure that 33 is nine panes of sidewalk. Then it's over.

Even if standing inside the living room, one can't be sure whether the house is occupied or not. The owner could be upstairs, napping on the floor.

0

If you want to know for sure, ask the walls.

There are partial handprints and a horizontal black line scuffed on one wall at about the height of a couch. Meaning there is a couch. Meaning there are people who throw themselves on it and mambo sideways into the wall. That would explain the handprints too.

Or meaning there was a couch

She realizes that she's crossed over from negating a presence to explaining an absence.

0

Faye can't say any of this to Denise, who is so *la di da* on the subject, but she feels like she could be robbed, raped, gang raped, strangled, mutilated, and strung up from the banister any day now.

0

Next time the subject comes up, Denise says that Faye should just sell the house and move.

"I just moved in. I'm not going to let Petrus run me from my land."

"Petrus?"

"From *Disgrace*. Coetzee." Denise and Faye were in a book club together. But that's not how it went down.

0

Denise is married with kids to look after. Faye is single. Spending the night isn't really an option. Plus they're not that close.

and there were people who threw themselves backward on it to watch TV, then settled trays of food on their laps and ate with their hands. That would also explain the traffic of handprints.

0

Might be an urban legend, but for what it's worth: there once was a woman in BC whose house was always untidy she suffered a stroke couldn't find the phone and ants ate her up completely.

Or her dog did. Or a man died as he was reaching for the knob of the front door.

It doesn't matter. Point is people die alone in their houses all the time.

0

The empty room lets itself go after everyone goes. It lights up a cigarette, reads the paper on the windowseat with pound cake and coffee. The cat wakes up, laps some water, and does yoga.

One night Faye calls her and asks her to pick up some pills.

When Denise delivers them, after dropping her son home from baseball, Faye opens the door slackly and walks back to her chair. The pills rattle as Denise follows her.

Faye sits near a dim lamp, hand to her forehead, in a washed-out blue robe. When she looks up, her lips are dry, her cheek covered with sun spots.

Denise wants to ask, *What happened?* But maybe this is how Faye looks without makeup.

"Could you bring me a glass of water?"

The sink is full of dishes, none of the cupboards holds glasses or plates at all.

"Thanks Lucy," Faye says to Denise, brushing cobwebs from her forehead.

Denise notices.

Everyone, the whole street, is gone to work, the kids to daycare. The couples don't kiss goodbye anymore. The wife is too afraid to ask the husband to start kissing her again, in front of the kids, when he comes down for breakfast like husbands and wives do in any normal sitcom family, because he might say something worse than *no*, like *why?* or *there's too much of you to kiss*, and she would have to avoid herself in the reflective appliances, the windows, the warping utensils.

Walls absorb all of that. They're worse than children. They need an outlet.

0

But the facts: 33 was up for sale, then the sign came down.

III

000

PRELUDE

Because she has no one to play with, Raq plays piano four, five hours an evening. Soon as she comes home, she heads straight for it, the piano, leaving the door open for her younger brother Dee who bothers with the mail and the deadbolts and neatening up their boots.

Dee microwaves dinner, split pea soup their father prepares on Sundays and freezes. He spoons out his share, leaves Raq's in the kitchen, and settles in front of the TV with volume three, *Byzantine to Confucius*, of an encyclopedia open beside him. Raquel will reheat her bowl of soup when she's made some progress on — what, Chopin still? She's just coming off a Bach phase, months and months of ivy fugues climbing every which way. Yes, it's Chopin. Bach would sprout by now. This melody sputters like a spark lighter.

About an hour later, Raq flicks Dee's ear as she crosses behind him on her way to the kitchen. Progress. She's memorized a section. She comes back to the piano, puts her bowl on the bench, on top of Czerny's *Practical Finger Exercises*, and continues playing.

A couple of spoonfuls. Play. Another spoonful. Play. And so on until the soup is gone.

"Dee, you want to hear it?" she shouts from the other room.

"I'm hearing it."

She plays the first half of the piece from memory.

"Should be faster," he says when she's done. He's no expert, but he has a gravity so uncommon for his age that people take him seriously.

"Like this?" Raq begins the prelude again, slightly faster. "It says *lento*, though."

Raq can't see Dee read straight from the encyclopedia, which he finds more charming than the Internet for winter afternoons: "Chopin intended *rubato* to be played with a slight hesitation in the right hand while the left hand maintains a steady tempo."

"Really?" She repeats the first nine bars.

There is no saving that one-chord melody. *Spark spark spark*, nope. *Spark spark spark*, nope.

Raq's bowl, crusting with dried split peas, stays on top of Czerny until she hears a car in the driveway, then she scrambles to the kitchen. Dee turns off the TV and starts on problems from an infantile math textbook. Raq takes a seat across from him at the dining table and starts on hers.

0 0 0

If Raquel ever makes it big, *big* as far as concert pianists go, her mother will have a good story, like the mothers of Lang Lang, who first heard classical music on *Tom and Jerry*, and Evgeny Kissin, who hummed Bach at eleven months: *I took Raq to a dental appointment when she was about four, and she heard this music. I wasn't paying it any attention, because, you know, you get into*

*the magazines or whatever. But she, she was completely hypnotized
by it. She kept asking, What's the song? What this song? Well,
I didn't have a clue so I asked the receptionist* who asked the dentist
who scribbled the name down for the receptionist who told Raq's
mother who told Raquel that it was Rachmaninoff.

"Was I named after him?" Raq asked.

"No," her mother said and went back to *People*.

o o o

The next afternoon, Raq and Dee repeat the previous one, except
split pea soup morphs into split pea burritos. It's winter in Winnipeg.
Raq opens the house with the key around her neck, she sheds her
knapsack, mitts, coat on the way to the piano, waits for the door to
bang, the slap of mail on the table, then begins fondling the melody
to Prelude 13. She loops the second page, takes a break for her homework when a car crunches snow in the driveway, then loops through
preludes one to thirteen until she goes to bed, and even then, the
melodies still break on her like waves after a day in the sea.

Dee says from the other room, "It's the same note — "

"Chord."

"Chord, whatever, over and over again. It's like he was stuck
that day." Sports commentator voice: "Day thirteen, Chopin's got
nothing."

"It's too subtle for you."

"How many times can you repeat the same chord? Play something else."

" It's not about repetition. It's about persistence." Raq loops back
to the top of the second page. "When you're older maybe."

"It's boring." Dee prefers pieces *con fuoco*. "Same thing in the
left hand." Dee sings, "♪♪♪♪, ♪♪♪♪."

Thirteen is an easy prelude, technically, for Raquel. The F-sharp key doesn't throw her, neither does the double pedalling, the softer than soft *pianissimos*, not even the *legato* chords at the top of the second page. She can play it all except for two chords at the end. She plays from the top, trying to sneak up on the big chords, but they keep slipping from her grip.

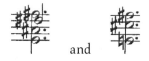 and

Dee enters with the *Saprophyte-to-Sumac* volume of the encyclopedia set.

"I can't get a couple of the chords at the end," Raq says. To show him, she puts her thumb on E, her second finger on A-sharp, her fourth on D-sharp, her fifth dangles short of F-sharp.

"Where?" Dee puts his hands on the piano and she directs his fingers to the one white key and three black keys. He can't play all notes simultaneously either. But he's ten.

"Listen to this," he says. "Robert Schumann."

"What about him?"

"Schumann is said to have devised an instrument to develop greater independence of the fingers." Dee is part reading, part telling. "It was some kind of finger-stretching device. Others claim that he cut the tendon shared by the third and fourth fingers. Left his right hand crippled."

"That's almost as bad as Beethoven."

o o o

Raq urges her mother to drop her off at her piano lessons half an hour early because she likes listening to a hulking seventeen-year-old boy pound his way through Rachmaninoff. He's been at the second concerto since January. In the spring recital, he'll play the solo piano part and Mr. Wakowski will play a piano transcription of the orchestral score.

Over the Christmas holidays, Mr. Wakowski separated his living room into two smaller rooms, joined by double doors. On one side you wait, on the other you play. The waiting room is crowded with oversized floral furniture and gauzy paintings of music lessons. The piano room has two pianos, a baby grand and an upright. When Mr. Wakowski gets annoyed, he demotes you to the upright and takes the baby grand to show you how it's done.

The secret is Raq has a crush on the Hulk. She will forever associate the word *passion* with him, because all the piano mothers fan themselves in the summer and say it over her head. *Passion* this, *passion* that. If she can impress him with her playing, he will marry her, so her twelve-year-old logic goes, and they will live in a house like Mr. Wakowski's with two pianos, and she will play the solo part and he the accompaniment. Dee says it's possible, anything's possible, but she shouldn't get pregnant or married until after high school. He printed out online copies of the second concerto so Raq could follow along while the Hulk plays.

The Hulk's coming up to the march in the first movement that sounds a bit like a polka.

It's Raq's favorite part; it breaks after a lot of swelling and drum rolling, and rides over the theme with four-note chords in each hand, eight fingers used up. *Pom* is the syllable she uses to hum along.

Her teacher suddenly emerges from the other side of the double doors.

"Keep playing, I'm listening," Mr. Wakowski says over his shoulder to the Hulk. He smiles at Raq on his way to the toilet. He seems to be having piss problems, is what she calls it, because he leaves urgently, sometimes twice, during her hour as well. From the waiting room, she can hear the liquid splash in the toilet. And a dribble afterward. A little moan. More dribbling.

On his way back, Wakowski sees that Raq has the concerto score open on her lap.

"Rachmaninoff is man's music." He is so enraptured by the Hulk, his head dances. "You need man's equipment."

Then she's alone in the waiting room again, listening to the two men play.

o o o

Her piano lesson goes by without event. Mr. Wakowski seems spent by the time he gets to her. He comes back from walking Hulk to the front door and says her playing is accurate to the point of sounding mechanical.

"Too much Bach," he says. "It's my fault. I have ruined you."

Then he's in the bathroom again.

In Dee's bedroom that evening, Raq says, "He thinks I don't know?"

She's tripping on her hands again. Raq can play fast, she can play loud, but she can't play everything. Her hands are too small.

"Apparently Mozart had tiny hands," Dee says. He has five browser windows open.

"And Rachmaninoff could span a thirteenth. What's your point?"

"Maybe your hands aren't the problem. Maybe it's your soul Wacky's talking about."

Raq glares at him. "It's a technical problem," she says syllabically.

"Then turn yourself into a Helen Keller, a Terry Fox." Dee holds a fist to his mouth and puts on a documentary voice. "Raquel Larson, she beat all odds to [pause, pause] reach her dreams."

Raq clouts him on the back of the head and goes downstairs to practice until one of her parents tells her that's enough. She consoles herself with the fact that her father used to play basketball. On her tenth, eleventh, and twelfth birthdays, she wished for her father's hand genes to kick in. Whenever she throws a penny into the mall fountain, right hand over left shoulder, correct form, she wishes for hands the size of palm fronds. When she finds a loose eyelash, when a clock lines up repetitions, *1:11*, *2:22*, and jackpot *11:11*, she wishes for her knuckles to drag along the floor. With wishes, as with anything else, persistence is key. All this she's thinking while playing

13.   But Dee's partly
right, the problem isn't so much the size of her hands; it's their reach. She could live with her hands if the web between her thumb and index finger wasn't so tight. Right now, she could span an octave easily enough, but if she stretches for some ninths or a tenth, her thumb hits two keys at the same time.

A few beats later, Dee comes down with their father's laptop and sits beside her on the bench. He stretches his right hand over the music to annoy her. He has the hands she wants, thumb joint like an adjustable wrench.

"How much would you give me for these paws?"

Raq goes back to the beginning.

He kneels on the bench and puts the laptop on top of the upright. There's an image of two splayed hands on the screen.

"I found a guy who had a hand transplant." Dee reads bits from the website. "First they fixed the bone, then they re-attached the tendons, arteries, nerves, and veins. Cool, eh." He imagines fitting the veins together like pushing one straw into another. "It's called a *composite tissue allotransplantation.* You'll have to go on immuno-suppressive drugs, otherwise your body will reject it. Like *The Addams Family.*"

"Then I'll have man hands," Raq says.

"So you game?"

No answer. She's trying to half-pedal part of the prelude.

"All right. How about this?" Dee opens a new window and types *web thumb surgery index finger* into a search engine and gets the term *thumb hypoplasia.*

"There's an operation," Dee says.

"Turn," she says.

Dee turns the page. "That separates thumbs when they're fused to index fingers."

"Time," Raq says.

"I don't know how long it takes. It's probably quick."

"I mean what time is it? Tell me when it's 5:55."

The taskbar says 5:53 p.m.

"You can wish all you want," Dee says, reading her mind —
he knows all about her squandering wishes on her hands. Then he
quotes their mother when she puts on makeup. "Sometimes nature
needs a little help."

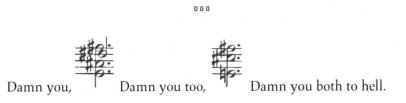

Damn you,   Damn you too,   Damn you both to hell.

The prelude turns into an obsession. By the time her next piano
lesson rolls around, Raq has the whole thing memorized, she
can play it in almost any key, and she's watched eight different
recordings online. Some performers can't manage the chord either
so they slur it. They disgust her. The tendon of her thumb hurts.
She's near asking Dee to make her a finger-stretching device like
Schumann's.

The Hulk comes out of his piano lesson sweating. Hair wet at
the edges, upper lip beaded, armpits a darker green than his shirt.

Mr. Wakowski says *passion*, says *vigorous*. The Hulk wipes his
forehead with the back of a muscular, meaty hand. Raquel stands
up and the Hulk takes her seat while he waits for his ride.

Raq figures she better do something to make Prelude 13 com-
pete with the Hulk's "vigorous," "passionate" interpretation of
Rachmaninoff's second concerto.

13.

"Too heavy," Mr. Wakowski says. "Start again. 1 2 3, 4 5 6."

"Raquel, tenderly, *teneramente*. Start again. 4, 5, and."

"Forget the left hand, let me just hear the right hand. And."

Then he calls for the Hulk. She's being demoted to the upright. The Hulk makes the melody sing, as if he's playing it on violin rather than piano. Mr. Wakowski's eyes flutter backward at the opening chords. By the top of page two, he's breathing through his teeth. By the handbreakers, "the heartbreak chords," he calls them, he's cross-armed, rubbing his hands up and down the sides of his body.

Raq takes her seat at the baby grand again. She is sitting in the steam of the Hulk. He smells like a hot shower.

"Yes," Wakowski says, his eyes closed. "Lightly. Yes. Tender. Easy. Do it like that."

The Hulk sucks in his breath when she slurs the heartbreaker. Now he'll never marry her.

Wakowski sings on, "Play it gently. Play it without touching the piano."

o o o

Dee's biggest concern for his sister is the anesthesia. They're huddled together searching online for pain medication. Neither of them has a credit card, so they can't buy, just research. Dee asked for a Visa for Christmas, promising to pay the bill out of his allowance but, of course, didn't get one.

"We can't get the real hospital anesthesia, so we'll have to use some herbal stuff."

Raq doesn't like the sound of that. It sounds like medieval Europe. Could herbal stuff conk you out?

"Why don't I just get high on glue and weed?" she says.

"Could you get weeds?" Dee imagines powdering the leaves then compressing the green mush into a pill or boiling it into a drink. He doesn't know much about street stuff. Neither does Raquel, to be honest. She's only heard some kids talking about smoking *not a cigarette, weed stupid. You even know what weed is?*

"We could get aspirin easy," Dee says.

"Not strong enough."

"Extra strength."

"Do you have any idea how painful this is going to be?"

"I could probably get bear tranquillizers from Uncle Edwin."

"I'm not a freaking animal, Dee."

"A simple sedative then. Sleeping pills, barbiturates, benzos."

He speaks with the offhand casualness of a doctor. "Take three, four pills, then you'll go to sleep.

"How do you know this stuff?" Raq says, then she notices that the links are purple. It isn't his first time visiting these sites.

"Then I'll do the surgery, then you'll wake up."

"When? What if I don't wake up?"

"I'll stick my finger down your throat."

"No."

"You'll puke up all the pills. It's not like you're going to die."

"No!" Raq is starting to whine like a teenager.

Dee searches some more. While scrolling down the page of a pharmaceutical company, he says, "It's a short operation anyway. Maybe you could just bear it."

Raq and Dee consider how they will explain the bandages on Raquel's hands ("burned myself heating up dinner," "I fell at school," "science experiment, Bunsen burner") but once the bandages come off, they'd be in deep trouble.

"Forget it," Raq says. "We can't pull it off."

Dee sees his chance to practice some real science slipping away, his sister back at the piano banging away in frustration, and he thinks they have come too far to quit, the solution is too close.

So he says, "I'll take the blame."

She looks at him like he's Jesus.

o o o

They decide on Dee's bedroom for the operation because of its "emotional sterility." Together, they spend days after school getting the details right. Dee wants a pair of tiny silver scissors. "The tip is important," he said. He wants a non-toxic marker. After school, they buy all the supplies with their allowances and stash them in the bottom drawer of Dee's night table. At home they find gauze, rubbing alcohol, bandages, a boxcutter, and they plan to make an icepack by stuffing ice in a sandwich bag.

Dee's most proud of a device he creates out of wire, which is like a pair of scissors held open. Raquel will slip her thumb and index finger into the two rings which will spread open the web of her hand and prevent her from moving her fingers during the operation. Dee calls it, using his commercial voice-over voice, *the webspread.*

The afternoon of the operation, they have their regular two-hour window before their parents come home. Their father will be home first this afternoon. He'll meet Dee watching TV. Raquel will have turned in early because of cramps. Their father's still new to the whole menstruation thing so he'll probably just stand outside Raq's door and ask if she's okay. In the morning, according to plan, Raq and Dee will come clean if necessary.

Raq puts on her mother's eye mask and lies down on Dee's bed. Dee plugs in large earphones, their father's, to Raq's stereo, temporarily relocated to his room, and places them over her head. Total sensory deprivation. Raq won't see or hear any snipping. And it shouldn't feel too bad either. She downed an Aspirin, a Tylenol PM, and two tablespoons of NyQuil before lying down, plus Dee already applied ice and a topical anesthetic cream to each of her hands.

Dee waits until she is nearly asleep before completing Raq's pre-operative care. He slides the fingers of her right hand into the webspread. He puts plastic bags under her hands to keep her blood off his sheets. Seeing her lips relax, he realizes he should have thought of himself during the procedure. He should have erected a sheet to cut her off at the hand, or maybe just thrown a blanket over her whole body. Her forearm is here, her fingernails, her wrist bone. She is still here. He wants to be separate from her pain, cut her like an earthworm, not like a human. A vein forks on the back of her hand.

He should have thought about music for himself, so he couldn't hear the snowplow outside, the ordinariness of the wind through the window screen.

The topical anesthetic should have kicked in by now. All he has to do is snip along the line he drew along a crease.

He opens the silver scissors over her flesh, and squeezes. Just like a chicken breast his mother would cut over the sink, only blood. Raquel tenses up. Her consciousness runs down her arm before it circles back to her mouth. Her hand tries to close into a fist but the webspread prevents it.

"Dee!" Raq tries to stop him with her left hand, but it's clumsy in the webspread.

"Almost done, almost done."

Dee grabs her left hand, places his knee on her wrist to hold it still to the mattress, then opens the little beak and bites. He dabs it with a cotton ball, lifts the cotton to look at it, he wants to cut a little deeper, but Raq is fully up now. Crying.

"Dee! Stop! I don't want to do this. I can't — "

"All done. We're done." Then he goes for it and clips the left hand more. He has to cut through blood. "Now I'm done."

He squeezes the cotton on her left hand. "All done."

With the eye mask on, Raq tilts her head back as if blind. She is also panting.

"We're done, Raq. I'm icing it, then I'll dress it. *Shh, shh,* it's okay, we're done, *shh.*"

000

The car radio is loud. A morning show. A man speeds through the traffic report. Raq and Dee are in the back seat of the Chrysler as their mother speeds to Emergency although the roads are icy this morning. Their mother on her cell phone berates their father, "Didn't you check on her last night? If this is what you call responsible parenting, then — I don't care. You can talk about stepping up all you like, but being a parent means more than bloody mashed potatoes and enchiladas."

One of Raq's bandages is open, the other is blotted with blood.

Their mother slaps the phone closed. "How could you be so stupid, Raquel?"

No answer.

But in their mother's voice, Raq can hear her mother blaming herself for not being home enough. Raq and Dee had calculated the timing to correspond with a double shift, when their mother's abandonment complex peaks.

"You're the older one, Raquel. If Dee told you to slit your wrists, would you do it?"

Now she's talking crazy.

"Deform yourself like that." Their mother's dialing again. Her voice changes when a new caller picks up. "Yes, this is Julie Larson. I'm calling to let you know Raquel and Dee Larson won't be in school this morning. Raquel's in Mrs. Singh's class. Dee's in — yes, that's right."

They pull into St. James hospital, where Julie works. At least everyone there knows she's not a bad mother. Everyone knows she wasn't home. She walks right through triage and finds Dr. Hollenbeck leaving a patient, pulling a curtain closed behind him.

There are no rooms, as usual. He sits Raquel on a stretcher in the corner and examines her cut webs. Behind the curtain someone is vomiting. Someone else is moaning a long, steady dial-tone moan.

"It's not bad, Julie. What do you want me to do?"

"Fix it," she says like the hysterical patients other nurses mock.

"I could stitch it up like it was before, but that's just going to traumatize the area, well not *traumatize*, but why put her through that?" He yawns. It's 8:15. This is his eighteenth hour of work. "Or I could have someone clean it and bandage it properly. You could do that. Grab yourself some antibiotics."

Their mother wants more.

"Really, Julie, the incisions are done pretty well. No veins cut, no tendons. It's just skin basically."

Dee tries not to smile.

"She's disfigured, mutilated."

"When it heals, it's nothing people are going to notice. It's not going to end her piano career by any stretch. It might even — "

Seeing the mother's shock at having him condone what she considers butch surgery, the doctor says something responsible. "Look, I can close them up."

Raq and Dee exchange looks behind their mother's back. The doctor notices.

"But the best thing," Dr. Hollenbeck says, "is to make another incision then close each half with stitches."

The mother wants more.

"And cleaning it is going to sting too."

More.

"Raq, if you want to be a concert pianist, don't let anyone mess with your hands, okay, not even professionals. Hold still. This is going to hurt."

Almost.

"And now, you amateur surgeon, you've got to promise to lay off the surgeries until you go to med school, okay?"

Dee nods and tries to look penitent.

Enough.

In the car home, their mother doles out punishment like confetti.

Three weeks. A month. No TV. No Internet. No nothing. You come straight home and do homework until it's time to go to sleep. No piano. (Good, thinks Raquel, my hands will heal.) No music. No books, Dee. You hear me. Their mother reconsiders. No good books. No encyclopedias. No books outside of school.

Later that evening, when their father comes home, the house is quiet. He looks at Raq's bandaged hands. He raises his voice, but the long drive home, the overtime, has taken the spontaneity out of whacking Dee. He slaps on two weeks to their sentence just to show how mad he is. It's really a gesture to his wife, an apology for his negligence.

The first night of their incarceration, Dee reminds Raq that she will feel some post-operative depression. He is summoning everything he can remember from the web.

When she's alone, the Schumann story comes back, a career ruined by ambition. Her thumb already feels less sensitive. Maybe Dee cut a nerve, maybe her thumb is turning to a black gangrenous stub under the gauze. How could she let a kid operate on her hands? At school, she'll have to walk around basically in mitts. The girls will call her *retard*. They'll say, *Hey Beethoven*, the only composer they know, *catch*, and throw things at her.

Dee's right again, the feeling passes after a few days. Her mother removes the bandages soon after. Dee looks at it and suggests some post-operative reconstruction to make it more elegant. He says he could tidy up Dr. Hollenbeck's work. There is definitely less skin there, but her thumb barely stretches further, like lions in a cage or circus elephants, trained not to go too far. But there is potential.

Raq doesn't want to disturb her hands. She treats them like dolls. It looks kind of cool, she thinks, like she's a girl with a secret, a cutter, an anorexic. She's a girl with a story.

Dee would have to thank her as much as she thanked him. During those weeks, he decides not just to be a doctor, not just a surgeon either, but a reconstructive surgeon.

"I've been reading about nose jobs," he says, coming into her room. He's been sneaking time on the Internet.

"Keep reading."

"I don't have exactly the right facilities. You think I can rent surgical space? A clinic after hours."

"Why don't you ask Dr. Hollenbeck?" She's reading the second movement of the Rachmaninoff concerto.

"You can keep the ethnic shape, I'll just —" He takes out a dry Popsicle stick from his pocket and moves it toward her nose. She tries to brush him away, but he's determined. He leads her to her mirror.

"First I'll raise the bridge here with a silicone implant." He pokes her nose upward. "Then maybe suck out some fat from the tip, and reduce the flare of the nostrils." He takes a second Popsicle stick and forms a triangle at the base of her nose. "It's all pretty easy."

He looks at her in the mirror, asking her what she thinks with his eyes.

"There's no way you're touching my nose." She goes back to the bed and lies on her back so that her head hangs off the side of the bed, which gives Dee an idea.

"How about a boob job?"

Raq throws a pillow at Dee and he closes the door behind him just in time. Raq puts down the score and wonders if the Hulk likes girls with big boobs. She hasn't seen him in a month. No piano, according to her mother, also means no piano lessons. By the time she gets back, the Hulk and Mr. Wakowski will be slamming through the third movement.

So Raq and Dee pass the slow six weeks by making a little joke of it, because they won, after all. Raq draws an X through each day. Dee tallies them on the wall underneath his bed. She prepares for her release by reading through the Rachmaninoff concerto and memorizing the rest of the Chopin preludes. Like Glenn Gould, who could perform a piece from memory right after studying the score, she plans to play the entire cycle from memory once she's allowed to touch the piano again.

Man hands, she thinks. *I'll show you man hands. With these babies, my Chopin days are coming to an end. Bring on the Rach.*

The morning of freedom, Raquel announces her return triumphantly with the biggest, loudest handbreaking chord-playing the house has ever heard.

Blam!   *Blam!*   *Blam!*   *Blam!*

0 0 0

When Raq lets herself in forty-five minutes early, she hears only the solo piano part. There's no accompaniment. Mr. Wakowski's probably in the bathroom. Before he returns, she figures she can take a peek at the Hulk banging chords—third movement, she knows exactly where he is from her weeks of reading. She puts her *Complete Preludes* down on a flowery chair and opens the door enough to see with one eye.

She is not sure what she's seeing at first. The way they are put together, she thinks she is watching a mutant. The Hulk has four legs, two of which are kneeling, his head is thrown back, his mouth open, his Adam's apple trembling.

A blur of fingers.

Raq closes the door, goes back to her seat, and waits her turn. Music surges. A blur of. She sits on her hands.

CARDIOLOGY

Bella was cutting up a cardboard box for her daughter when the phone rang.

"Who? You've got the wrong number," she heard Riley say. "There's no bells here." And that brought Bella running.

"Shane, that you?"

Riley took the scissors from her mother.

This might have been the first time Shane had called, but he and Bella had been swapping chummy emails since he found her on oldclassfriends.com, then they upgraded to instant messaging, then texting, and now apparently to the phone call, which could only mean that soon enough they'd

"You're where?" Bella said. And knowing Shane, no doubt he wanted to go out. But that evening, Bella couldn't. For real.

"Me and Riley are working on her project. It's pretty big. I—" she sucked in her breath. "I can't, Shane."

"Oh come on, comeon comeon comeon."

"Really, I can't. But you can hang here if you want." And so that he couldn't refuse without being a prick, she added:

"I mean that's if you don't mind hanging with a fourth grader."

Riley quit cutting and stood in front her mother, arms akimbo, hard to miss. She read her mother's body — the inclined head, the finger sliding back and forth along her collarbone, the little girl voice — and knew this man, this *Shane* who calls her mother *Bells*, could seriously mangle her evening.

Bella put her hand over the mouthpiece and mouthed, "Tidy up."

Riley wanted to swing a racket hard, hard through her mother's face.

o o o

Shane didn't need a reason to go out. He just preferred to be with his friends to staying at home, watching TV with his family. Some people are like that, right? They prefer to be outside, doesn't matter where, than at home; eating restaurant food instead of their mothers' potatoes. From the time he was fourteen, Shane's family, for the most part, gave up trying to track him.

"You don't know? How could you not know where you're going?"

"I just told you, Mom, me and Bells are going to hang out."

"Where's Bella then?"

"I don't know."

"So how are you going to find her?"

"Relax, I'll find her."

"Where, Shane? Where?" He wrung her heart dry back then.

And now that Shane was in his mid twenties, he carried on the same way whenever he came home. He'd wake up in the afternoon, eat handfuls of cereal, watch some Court TV, shower, slap on cologne, step into his shoes, and at the door, car keys in hand, he'd say, *I'm going out for a minute.*

Sitting dazed in front of the TV, back straight in a wooden chair, his mother listened to his movements upstairs, and waited for his *I'm going out for a minute*. When the car drove off, hers, some old film would crackle inside her. She'd look inward, sit motionless a few minutes, then suddenly squint at the TV to figure out what she was watching, the original program long finished, before flipping to the channel where the program listings scrolled.

Because of what it did to their mother, that tiny moment when their mother got lost in her privacy, Shane's sister hated it when he came home.

0 0 0

Shane entered Bella's apartment with his torso thrown back as if carrying boxes much larger and heavier than the two pizzas he had picked up. He paused at the mess of cardboard and construction paper around Riley.

"So what're you working on?"

Riley turned to see if he was worthy of a response, then turned away. "It's for school."

"It's her Science Fair project," Bella said from the kitchen.

"Oh yeah? What's it about?"

Riley knelt upright behind the coffee table. "I'm measuring the effects of chocolate on the heart rate and blood pressure of a twenty-six-year-old woman."

"You've got a little cardiologist on your hands," he said to Bella. Then to Riley, "That's pretty advanced stuff for a fourth grader."

"Not really," Riley said. "Marcus Avery is building a flying car."

"Would you stop with Marcus Avery," Bella said. She spread three plates, three glasses, a roll of paper towels, and a two-litre bottle of Coke on the coffee table. "Tell Shane your hypothesis."

"That heart rate and blood pressure will go up."

/ 179 /

"And?"

"And if you keep eating chocolate, eventually your heart will explode."

Shane made a face.

"Show him your graphs, Riley."

Shane looked at one, then the other, then both side by side, then separately again. Not that there was much to analyze, just four dots sloping upward slightly.

"What?" Riley said.

"Nothing. It's just… mm."

"What?" She folded her arms.

Oh please no, Bella thought, she's just a kid, don't knock her project. Came up with the chocolate idea on her own — well, she saw a spot on TV, but still. She's never worked harder on anything.

"I mean it's good and all, but you only have four dots."

"It's due tomorrow, Shane," Bella intervened. "We don't have time for anything fancy."

"Here's what I'm proposing." He went into MBA mode. "You could double your results if you added one more person." He pointed two thumbs at himself. "Your hypothesis could be something about the heart rate of a twenty-six-year-old man *and* woman. What do you think? You want to put Marcus Avery to shame or what?"

"Well," Riley said.

And with that, Shane knew he had made the sale.

"You're both old."

o o o

Shane's sister, Nora, and her husband bought a house down the street from her parents. Her father was getting old in the most predictable ways: hypertension, high cholesterol, wheeziness, and a phlegmy old-man cough. Her mother's arthritis had turned her into a winter tree, sapped what little spunk she had, dried up her skin.

When Shane visited this time, only because their father was in the hospital, he said he wanted to stay with Nora, check out the new house, help with the kids, when really he didn't want to be pulled under by his mother's endless reminiscing.

He lasted one night at Nora's place.

No one knew his flight details. *Don't worry about it. I'll get someone to pick me up.* He, duffel bag, and friend arrived boisterously in the evening. He dropped his bag on the couch, farted his lips on the kids' bellies, slapped Dan on the back, opened the pot, closed it, changed his shirt in front of everyone in the living room, and left with his friend.

"I'm going out for a minute."

Long minute. When Dan and Nora turned in, he wasn't back yet. Next day Nora told him straight up she had two young kids to watch out for and he couldn't be coming in any time of the night.

"What does one thing have to do with the other?" Shane asked.

How could she explain to a bachelor who'd never had more than a four-month relationship the trouble of getting a five-year-old and a nine-month-old to sleep, how to her son any night noise was sure sign of a monster, and that if he heard the door open he'd call *mommy mom mommy mooom* until she—not Dan—airlifted him to their bed, and how in the morning, she'd have to find answers for *why does Uncle Shane sleep so late?* and *how come Uncle Shane doesn't have to eat a boiled egg?* Not to mention Dan's disdain for slobs, MBA aside, who party all night and can't wake up at 7:30 like self-respecting members of the workforce.

Shane looked at Nora as if she had broken the sibling pact, converted to the cult of parenthood.

"Fine," he said, "I'll stay with mom."

"I'm not asking you to leave."

"No, no, I mean if I'm causing trouble in your house, I'll go." He left the box of cereal on the table and went upstairs.

Daughter on her hip, Nora put the box away. *Really, would it kill him to clean up?* She wet a towel and wiped down the kitchen table. *Really, would it?*

Shane came down with his duffel bag, finishing up a conversation with their mother on his cell phone. "Are you gonna be home? I can take care of it now if you want."

The baby started fussing on Nora's hip. Shane simply plugged his exposed ear.

"I'm going to help Mom fill up her coolant," he said to Nora, leaving the room. What had Nora been doing all these years, he was implying, letting Mom drive an overheating car?

o o o

Shane was narrating while Riley typed.

"Purpose: To test the effects of chocolate on the heart rates —"

"Slow down. Of choc- o- late- on the- heart- rates."

"and blood pressure of a twenty-six-year-old couple — no, twenty-six-year-old male and female. Got that?"

"Male- and- fe- male. Yeah."

"Hypothesis. "

"I think mom will win."

"Hypothesis: The heart rate and blood pressure of the man will increase faster, meaning his heart will explode first. I'm kidding. Don't type that last part."

"I like it."

"All right, materials: stethoscope and the blood pressure thing, the pump."

"Mom, how do you spell sphygmomanometer?"

"S-p-h-y-g, mom, man, o, me, ter."

o o o

"He's the only brother you'll ever have, Nora."

"I didn't throw him out, okay."

Gladys thought of her daughter's situation — the needy little boy, the over-attached baby, always on her hip, and sympathized. "Shane should give up those late nights now. Remember the summer he bought the Chevy?"

This story again. Shane got a part-time job after he got his license, saved all his money, bought a cheap cheap two-door Chevrolet Cavalier, packed his friends into it, came home after midnight all summer, eventually crashed the car one evening his mother told him not to go out, broke his leg, went crazy hobbling around the house.

"Learned his lesson," Gladys said.

Nora would disagree.

They were having this conversation in a couple of hospital chairs beside Walter's bed. Nora was slouched in her seat, hands laced on her belly. Her mother, erect, ankles crossed, took the mail out of her handbag to sort. They couldn't talk like this in front of Shane. Not that they were afraid of him, but he had this way of making their voices sound like mosquitoes, even to themselves, when he got into MBA mode. *What does one thing have to do with the other?*

A nurse came in with some pills for Walter. All three of them knew their parts: the nurse woke him, Nora raised him, Gladys put his glasses on his eyes.

"Shane gone?" Walter said after he had swallowed.

/ 183 /

"When you fell asleep."

"He waited for a while," Gladys covered. "You've been out for half an hour now."

Danced in and tussled with his father as if he weren't sick, insisted on letting him get into the wheelchair himself — *You guys fuss too much over him. See, he's strong. Aren't you, champ* — then wheeled him around the ward, took him away from the women, because clearly they were making him sick with their solicitous hovering.

"Mind over matter," Shane said when Walter fell asleep.

"He had a heart attack, you quack," Nora said.

"Kids."

"See it's that kind of negativity that's going to keep Dad sick. You have to talk positive around him."

Nora was pissed. Shane didn't even know what was going on. He saw their father one day, hadn't spoken to a doctor, didn't even know the nursing staff, but was somehow set to prognosticate a full recovery. And what the hell was up with *champ*?

Shane yawned. "I'm going to head home for a minute and have a nap. What time do visiting hours finish?"

"Don't worry about that." Gladys remembered her son's situation — the long flight, the important client he was stalling to be here — and sympathized. "Nora can bring me home."

o o o

The three of them were sitting on the floor, backs against the couch, pizza crusts on plates, quarter glasses of Coke.

Forty minutes in, everyone had the procedure down. When Shane's watch beeped, Riley would give three squares of chocolate to Shane and her mother, which they would suck to liquid.

"You can't chew it," Riley said.

"Suck it," Shane said to Bella. "You have to suck it."

Next Riley would whip out the stethoscope, measure beats per minute.

"You could get a reading from the pulse," Shane said, but Bella invented some reason to let Riley continue playing doctor.

Next came the sphygmomanometer, then finally dots on the graph — blue for Shane, red for Bella, who had used the experiment as an excuse to change into a low-cut tank top. Shane had rolled his sleeve all the way up to his freshly gymned bicep.

"What's it say this time?" Shane said. Trial 5. "Am I flatlining?"

"You went up to 100," Riley said. She had her finger on the last dot. "Mom's at 85."

They had started with resting heart rates of 71 for Shane, 62 for Bella. The blood pressure readings were the disappointing part. Riley thought the sphyg was broken. Shane thought, but didn't say, that Riley didn't know how to use it.

Plan was to run twenty trials, one every ten minutes, which meant a hundred and twenty squares of chocolate, three hours, ten minutes altogether, and an end time of 10:10 p.m. Not bad. Between trials, they had the business of the display board to take care of. They had already typed up *Purpose, Hypothesis, Materials,* and *Procedure. Observations, Conclusion,* and *Application* had to wait until later. To fill up the rest of the backboard, Riley was planning to print pictures of hearts off the Internet and cut out a bunch of Hershey kisses from foil. At the moment, she was busy tracing the letters of the project's title, CHOCOLATE HEARTS, with all the Os in the shape of kisses.

Shane and Bella had their own jobs. Bella manned all cutting apparatus — scissors, pinking shears, boxcutter — while Shane was in charge of all gluing and sticking applications, bristol board on cardboard, printouts on construction paper; he would administer white glue, glue stick, glue gun, scotch tape, masking tape, electric tape as necessary. All decisions had to go through Riley. And she also had full authority over the glitter pens.

"Watch out Marcus Avery," Shane said when he finished gluing the last blue sheet of bristol board to the backboard. "So he your boyfriend or what?"

"Ew."

"It's not *ew*. Your mom had tons of boyfriends."

"I did not."

"And just what was Gary Hoover then?"

"That was high school, genius, not grade four." Bella handed him the *Purpose* and a sheet of red construction paper. "And we were never officially boyfriend girlfriend."

Shane's watch beeped.

"Like I would," Bella said.

000

The endless reminiscing started up in earnest after Walter was down again. Nora listened to her mother until they were both drowsy. Same stories evening after evening.

The one where Shane bought a Chevy, crashed it, broke his leg, and went crazy hobbling around the house all summer.

The one where Gladys proofread all of her husband's reports for the first ten years — he was such a bad speller. She was there pumping quietly, unnoticed, behind his first promotion.

The one where Gladys heard a crash downstairs and found Walter on the kitchen floor, mouth open, white pastry bag open, knife half under the stove, and called 911, then called Nora who came running down the street in her husband's shoes, and that first nurse who said, "We don't have beds in Coronary Care," and how Gladys took up drying his neck and checking the balance of his IV herself, and how Walter's body eventually relaxed like he was between contractions, counting toward the next wave of pain.

The one where Shane crashed his Chevy. Again.

o o o

Trial 7 heart rate scores: Shane 107, Bella still 85.

Blood pressure readings show little change.

At first they followed the results eagerly like an election. The MBA in Shane came out. He'd psych himself out while Bella was being tested, jump up and down like a boxer. Warned that he was skewing the integrity of the experiment, he said he was "actively pursuing" heart explosion, you know, to help Riley out with her hypothesis, and that technically it was the chocolate giving him the energy to air box, jog on the spot, re-enact kung fu films.

Maybe it was the chocolate, an aphrodisiac, people say, but Shane and Bella started passing messages to each other through Riley's project. When Shane's watch beeped, Bella said things like *Somebody pump me up.* Shane: *Time to be blown.* Bella: *Hit me, baby.* Shane: *You think it has a sister?* Bella: *Squeeze me.* Shane: *Feels nice and tight.* Riley couldn't understand what was so funny, except she didn't like how they were snickering, or trying not to.

It must have been around trial 9 or so that they got sloppy about being discreet in front of Riley. Shane's eyes lingered too long on Bella's body — we're talking milliseconds — her bra strap, the spaghetti straps over that, the texture at the bottom of her breasts, the disappearing head of the stethoscope. Worse, Riley noticed her mother falling into a daydream over Shane's upturned forearm, the juicy vein inside his elbow.

While he was being cuffed into trial 10 or 11, Shane surveyed the room seriously for the first time as if contemplating moving in.

o o o

Both Nora and Gladys fell asleep in their chairs. The stories were still going in Gladys's head. Lately, she had been replaying, involuntarily, one scene, the same old crackly film.

When she was pregnant with Shane, Walter used to come home from work all excited with a treat from the bakery for her and baby. One evening, he had a cinnamon roll — Gladys remembered the cinnamon roll — which they unrolled and shared on the bed. She was reading a lot in those days. Mostly Jane Austen, for some reason.

They were no different from most couples. They lay on their sides, propped on one elbow, facing each other, eating toward the best part. He was loosening his skinny tie, when one of them, must have been Gladys because she was the one who had always been concerned with such things, asked, "Which of us do you think will die first?"   [*Gladys*

And Walter answered as many men have: "I hope we both die at the same time. Car wreck."

"Plane crash," she matched him.

"Double heart attacks."

"Suicide pact."

Walter left the centre of the cinnaroll for   [*Gladys*

"You've got the edge anyway. Women usually outlive men." Then he added, "And all the men in my family have bad tickers."

"What if I die during labour, would you get married again?"
                                                [*Gladys*

Then the baby kicked. He was already named *Shane,* and had been restless inside her when she was talking but not when she was reading Jane Austen. Maybe *irritable,* not *restless.*

"I think he likes the cinnaroll," Gladys said. Maybe *restless.*

"Shane, buddy," Walter said to her stomach. "You like that? Or you want to get out? Hang in there, okay?"

"Mom." Nora's voice.

[Gladys

Walter had been wheezing her name.

"Gladys." The hair on his forehead was wet. Glady's stood up, dropping envelopes from her lap.

Nora ran for a nurse.

000

Last count, trial 14: Shane 116, Bella 78.

Blood pressure measurements were still messed up.

After that 9:10 trial, Riley started searching the Internet for hearts, the blood and veins kind, in her mother's room. She came out now and then with a printout for Bella to cut out. Mostly, though, Bella was carefully cutting tin foil into the shape of Hershey kisses to ornament the display board. Riley had no model, no flying car, so her backboard needed to be as flashy as possible, said Shane.

Less than an hour left, Bella's energy was beginning to wane, even with the chocolate. She had to work tomorrow. Shane was still abuzz with caffeine. The graphs told the same story.

"Was Gene official, Bells?" Shane asked.

"Mmhm," Bella answered quietly, not lifting her eyes from her cutting. "We were together for about four months."

"And the guy from soccer?"

"Sylvan Dennis. Mmhm."

"And Travis Fracchia?"

"Travis." She could barely pull up each face before Shane was on to the next one. "He used to flip his eyelids inside out to freak me out."

"And Paul the year above us?"

"Paul. Always in a — "

"And Francis Resch."

"Frankie."

"And the Kaz?"

"The Kaz."

"And — "

"Okay. I'm a whore. I get it."

o o o

In the elevator down to the Coronary Care Unit, Gladys noticed that the top of Walter's gown, not just his face, was damp with sweat. The porter couldn't care less. Walter's eyes were closed against the fluorescent lights. He looked like he wanted it all — the heart cramp, the lights, the open robe, the men touching him, the cool instruments — to be over.

But his hand, his hand was gripping the railing of the gurney so tightly the skin on his knuckles stretched translucent. His hand was hanging on — Gladys's eyes filled seeing it — to the steel rail. *For dear life, for the love of God, for the children, for heaven's sake, Walter.* Hair near the web of his thumb. The hand that snatched the last of the cinnaroll from her mouth, *Since I'm going to die first, I might as well.*

"Gladys?"

"What is it?"

He spoke so softly she had to put her ear to his mouth.

"Gladys, if I die — "

"We're in the hospital. You're not going to die." She remembered his skinny tie.

"I want you to — "

"Shh, Walter," Gladys said. Oh Lord, look at his hand fighting. "Don't say anything." She will not be a widow. She will not be left.

"Shane and Nora?" If he died now, those would be his last words. Give him ten minutes, twenty, a few more words, a last wish.

000

Joke came out wrong: "I'd call you more of an upscale escort."

Shane knew it was slipping out mistuned but it was too late.

Bella sucked in her cheeks and kept her head bent to her cutting. Twenty-six with a nine-year-old, no social life to speak of, gussied up in a tank top so tight you could see the texture of her bra.

"Joke," he said.

Bella stood up. "Riley, honey, I think it's almost time."

After the escort joke, Shane and Bella kept their conversation in the safe zones of their grade ten Bio teacher, graffiti on the portables, the table their group claimed in the caf. They both wished Riley was in the room more.

And Shane could no longer sell himself, not even to Riley, on whose likeability scale he had peaked at 70%. He felt his interest in her project, questions about the graph or the best glue for foil, tinkle with phoniness in front of her mother.

Bella 87, Shane — Who cares?

000

Nora stayed upstairs to deal with some paperwork.

"Why now?" she asked the nurse.

"Miss" was the answer she got.

She called Shane at their mother's house, trying to save him the roaming charges. The machine came on. Then she called Dan, who was watching the kids. He hadn't seen Shane. Then she called Shane's cell phone, which he never answered anyway when he saw her number.

She pinched the bridge of her nose.

Ring two, three, four.

o o o

After seventeen trials, Shane's phone vibrated across the coffee table.

"What's up?"

A woman, Bella thought.

"A friend's place."

I have a name.

"I don't know, whenever."

And she has you whipped.

Shane's expression crashed. "What happened?"

Without excusing himself, he walked to the balcony and closed the glass door behind him. *Definitely a woman.* He leaned on the railing, weight on one leg, and Bella observed the dough of his butt.

Whore A little taunt *whore* began in her head *hoah.* Reclining against the couch *hoah* she felt fleshy, more *hoah* Jabba the Hutt than Olympia *dirty hoah.*

She went to the bathroom to check her makeup. *Hoah.* Mascara was fine but her eyes were *hoah* turning red. The Kaz. *Hoah* More lip gloss. Why even bother? Bastard only wanted to *hoah* feel her up. Something to do. *Hoah.*

From the bathroom, Bella heard the front door close. She closed the medicine cabinet and left the bathroom.

Instinctively, she called for Riley. Riley was still at the computer.

"I heard the door," Bella said.

"Shane left."

"Why?" Bella looked around as if the reason would be on the walls of her bedroom.

Riley hummed *I don't know.*

"Didn't he say anything?"

"No. He was on the phone."

In her head, Bella smelled her armpits, cupped a hand to test her breath. Play it cool, she thought, no need for Riley to know her disappointment. Save that for the stethoscope. But a string of swear words played accordion in her mouth, joined at the *m* and *r* like the hands of a paper man chain.

Bella went back to the living room, resumed her position on the floor, back against the couch, and continued cutting. She noticed Shane's keys on the table, which meant he couldn't have gone far, which meant he had to come back. And he would come back for the trials anyway, Bella told herself. He wouldn't blow off Riley after he saw how serious she was about her little chocolate project. For Pete's sake, she was surfing the Internet for hearts.

"I made thirty kisses," she yelled to Riley. "How many do you want?"

Of course he was seeing someone. Guy like him, with a job, leather shoes. He didn't buy those himself.

Riley came into the room. "Mom, they're too big."

Bella looked down at her tinfoil kisses. They looked fine to her.

And, big deal, so he had a girl, just say that. Don't tell Riley you're going to do something then not do it.

If Shane could defend himself, he'd say, as he was fond of saying to women, *What does one thing have to do with the other?*

—Nora, calm down.

—BlahblahDYINGblahALREADY DEADblah

—Nora, what did the doctors say?

—BlahblahPAPERWORKblahblahSWEATING

—Nora, I can't talk to you when you're hysterical

—BlahGET YOUR BUTT DOWN HEREblahblahALREADY DEADblah

—Nora, just tell me what the doctors said.

—BlahblahI'M ALWAYS THE ONEblah

—Nora, cut the drama.

o o o

It was time for another trial. But Bella didn't mention it. She just glanced out the side of her eyes at Riley, who was back in the living room.

Riley studied the display board. She picked up a foil kiss. She set it on the board. She tilted her head. She moved the kiss over. She took it off. She flicked her finger under a shoddily glued item. She added a dab of glue. She placed a heart printout on the right side. Then, up through her spine, like a test your strength game, Shane and his watch shot to her brain.

"What time is it?" And before Bella could answer, Riley said, "We're late. It's time, it's time. Where is he?"

"Check the hallway."

She ran to the door, leaned out, and looked both ways. "Mom, I don't see him."

She closed the door.

The pump of the sphygmomanometer dragged along the floor behind her.

"Mom, tell him to hurry up."

"That's rude, honey."

"But he's going to screw everything up."

"Give him a minute. I'm sure he'll be back." Bella heard herself using her good-parent voice, and now she was about to use a good-parent strategy and redirect negative behaviour by offering a choice between two acceptable behaviours. She held up a resized foil kiss. "Do you want to stick this one over here or do you want to cut out some kisses yourself?"

But Riley could not be redirected. "Go get him."

Bella tried again. "Here, why don't you check me first, honey."

Bella wrapped the cuff around her own bicep. Riley began pumping absentmindedly. She was envisioning her project in flames, being stomped on, and Marcus Avery gloating demonically, a large blue ribbon being pinned on him like he was a prize cow. Her pumping had sped up, like her heart.

"Hey, take it easy. Sit down."

"Well go get him then." Riley now pumped deliberately, violently, threateningly. A tantrum was coming. "*Go* [chin thrust forward] *get* [her little teeth in neat white rows] *him*."

Bella's arm *Go* was about to *get* explode *him*.

"Riley! Stop it!" Bella pushed her daughter down with her free arm. "You're not going to win the friggin' Nobel prize."

Mistake. The velcro roared. Things a parent should never say.

Riley stayed on the ground a moment. Should she cry? She sorted her brain for things to say as she stood up. *Stupid project.* She saw the foil *stupid kisses* she was near tears *dumb hearts* she searched for something *I hope you both die* at the edge of language, something she picked up in school, the worst word she knew, although she wasn't completely sure of its meaning.

"Slut."

Partway through her conversation with Shane, Nora simply gave up. She let him tell her exactly what was going on in the hospital although she was there and he wasn't.

— Blahblahblahalarm him unnecessarilyblah

— You're right, Shane.

— Blahblaheverybody sweatsblahdoesn't mean he's dyingblah

— I guess I overreacted, Shane.

— BlahI'm right in the middle of somethingblahblah

— Do what you're doing, Shane.

— Blet the doctors do their workahblahblah

— Dad will be fine, Shane.

— He's toughblahblahyou and momblahalways so negativeblah

— Positive thinking, you got it, Shane.

As he was talking, Nora ran her finger along the hallway wall, down the stairs, all the way down to Coronary Care, and hung up.

He would be here if he wanted to be here.

Shane knocked on the apartment door and opened it long before anyone answered. This wasn't long after Riley had stormed into her room, five minutes tops. He sank down on the couch and rubbed his eyes.

Bella waited for an explanation.

He said nothing about the phone call.

He said nothing about the project.

He said nothing about the abandoned sphygmomanometer on the floor.

Bella only needed him for a few more trials. After that, she and

Riley, if Riley could be induced, would finish the gluing (his job) and the other decorative stuff.

Don't ask don't ask don't ask don't ask.

"Everything all right?" she asked in spite of herself.

He sighed.

But that was her limit. She would not beg him to extend the courtesy of information.

He sighed again, the righteous sufferer's sigh.

"Bells, I'm going out for a minute."

Bella didn't look up from trimming the foil kisses. He has some other woman around.

Shane wasn't fooled by her cool. He knew when women wanted to know more than he was giving, so to salvage the evening, he said, "That was my sister."

Whatever.

"There's an emergency."

Sure there was. Right, that long on the phone for an emergency. Real urgent.

"She's worried that my — "

"Don't tell me." Bella surprised herself.

He let his head drop in exasperation, tired of being reasonable with unreasonable people.

"You don't have to tell me." Spare me. "I mean, I don't want you to feel like you have to tell me."

He stood up to go, took a few steps toward the door, and only then remembered Riley. "What about the project?"

"We'll manage" without you.

o o o

Nora found her mother with her head on Walter's heart. Nora *dad um* mother *dad um dad um* Walter's heart.

"Goodness, Nora, where's your brother?"

Dad um, dad um, dad um dad um.

FALL

We first noticed the little corpses while duct taping the trees we
wanted to fell. Martha and I were so far into our forest that we
had lost sight of the house, where my father was putting our kids
to bed. The sky was turning navy. Blasts of wind tore dry leaves
from branches. In the dim light, the corpses looked like large
spruce cones on the ground. But when we shone our flashlights
down and turned them over with our shoes, we realized they
were birds.

We counted four that evening. A few days later, we counted
five. The same four plus one, I figured. Martha swore that all five
were fresh.

"How do you know that?" I said.

She crouched like a crime drama investigator and shot me
a look that said any rookie should know the difference between
a three-day-dead bird and a freshly dead one.

"Must be an avian disease," I said.

"How do you know that?" she quoted me.

"Har har."

Martha kept her investigator face on.

"You can't be serious," I said.

"How do you know they didn't die at the hand of a hunter, a sharp shooter, a serial bird killer?"

"There's no bullet wound, for one."

"Could be a fellow bird then."

"I don't think there are serial killers in the animal kingdom."

"And eagles and hawks would be?"

Martha had been debating too much with our three-year-old, Drew. Thank God Skip, our youngest son, couldn't talk yet. I looked to the sky for help.

"Killing for food doesn't make an animal a serial killer," I said.

"By that reasoning if a cannibal went on a killing spree then it would be okay."

We had started walking again, and we went on debating like this until we came across another bird, a tiny sparrow with brown and white streaks on its head. Its belly was swollen as if it had swallowed a plum. Martha lifted the sunglasses from her head.

"Don't touch it," I said.

She bent down and turned it over with the handle of her sunglasses. "It looks like Skip."

I couldn't see a resemblance. "It's an avian disease," I said finally. As I started toward the pond to tag some more trees, I told her I'd call the authorities and that she should stay inside until we knew for sure, or she should cover up at least. No opposition came from behind me, so I stopped and turned around. "Come on, let's go. We have another acre to cover."

"Don't you think it looks like Skip?"

"It's a bird, Martha. Animals don't look like people."

She stood up and shone her flashlight in my face. "Then how come you look like an ass?"

Skip's brother, Drew, walks across the back lawn toward him, wearing only boxers and construction boots. Drew's arms criss-cross his chest in what, from a distance, looks like an act of modesty, but as he gets closer to the family forest, is actually an attempt to keep his shoulders and triceps warm.

"You plan to fell trees like that?" Skip says.

Drew puts his thumbs into the elastic waistband, and wiggles his boxers down his hips like a stripper. The birds go *chickawahwah*.

"How many we got to do?"

"Three."

They're supposed to have all three trees felled by the end of the day, the wood split and stacked at the side of the garage. Last night, Skip had said they should start just after their parents leave for work, around seven, so they could get all the work done by mid afternoon. Drew was in front of his laptop, mouse in his right hand, phone in his left, texting. *Seven, Drew.* Skip said it like he was older. Yeah yeah. *Else I'm coming upstairs with the chainsaw over your bed.*

It's now twenty to eight. The birds go *chickawahwah*. Skip's ready to take the saw to something. Deep breaths, deep breaths.

Drew twists sideways to crack his back. "I only see two taped up."

"The other one's over by the pond. I already checked it out. It's not your birch."

"Dad's birch," says Drew. "I just keep it entertained. Know what I'm sayin." He stops near a tree and takes a leak, one fist on his hip. "Sick. This beetle's getting mad killed." And in falsetto to the beetle, he adds, "It's the flood. Run, run for your life."

"You realize we've lost forty minutes already," Skip says.

Drew shakes himself dry. "Let's get this pahty stahted." But he's walking the wrong way, back to the house, swinging his arms like a boxer loosening up.

o o o

During the fall of the dead birds, my father was still living with us. He had made himself and the boys invisible while Martha and I racked up money and property around New Hampshire. But we weren't WASPs. Compared to our neighbours, we were tightwads. We did our own yardwork and prepared our own firewood. And we cultivated the same New England work ethic in our boys, so when Drew and Skip got older, they would sometimes drive home from college for a weekend to help out.

That fall, they weren't nearly old enough to fell trees. They weren't even old enough to walk behind us and duct tape the ones we wanted felled.

From the beginning, there was a birch that Martha and I couldn't agree on. She said the dead birds were a sign that it was time for that birch to die.

"*Bird,*" she said, holding up one palm like a scale. "*Birch.*" She held up the other. "See?"

I didn't.

"They both have that *bir* sound."

More three-year-old reasoning. Her weakest argument yet. She didn't like the birch because it leaned and interrupted the attentive military formation of the other trees. I liked it because it formed an *A* with a tree behind it. One of its lower branches extended to make the bridge. Any trunk could substitute for an *l*, and we were halfway through my name. Plus, I had argued in the past, we need the leaning tree to define all the others. Over the years, I had sacrificed the lives of dozens of trees to save this one.

"This year it's got to go," Martha said. "Or it'll be hell for you."

"It's not diseased. Its roots are still — "

"No, Alan, no. I've had it. The tree comes down this year."

"Or what?"

"There's no *or*. It comes down, even if I have to hack it down myself."

I laughed. In the days before we had a chainsaw, when Martha was bra burning, I dragged her out of the house by the elbow, handed her an axe, and told her go ahead. She could barely even lift the axe, let alone swing it, let alone aim at the same spot. I had thrust my pelvis forward and joked that she should gnaw at it like a beaver.

Martha squeezed the coil of tape from her wrist where she was wearing it like a bracelet and unrolled about six inches. Then she smoothed it back on. The tip of her boot had mashed something soft.

Another bird.

Its head was a foot from its body.

o o o

It's after eight when Drew returns to get the "pahty stahted." He's dressed this time, as in he's wearing more than boxers, but compared to Skip, who's decked out in steel toe boots, protective Kevlar chaps, gloves, hard hat, goggles, and ear defenders, Drew might as well be logging naked.

"Where the chainsaw at?" Drew says. He's been talking like that — talking black, his parents say — since coming back from college. "I'll cut, you split. Shannon'll be coming over in a couple hours, so work fast, y'hear?"

Skip wants to remind Drew that he's the late one, but Drew yoinks his brother's goggles, revs up the saw, and cuts all talk.

o o o

Less than a week after the birch tree was spared for yet another year, Martha poured herself a glass of wine and sat on the couch, near the wood stove. She was distancing herself from the mess in the kitchen, the plate of butternut squash that Drew smashed so he wouldn't have to eat it. Immediately, my father snatched him and Skip out of their chairs — one to be punished, the other to watch and learn. But now, I was thinking that Drew had promising problem-solving skills. He couldn't eat food that was on the ground now, could he? What kind of parents allowed their kids to be punished for solving problems? I was explaining all of this to Martha, while picking up the broken plate, but she wasn't paying attention. Both her hands cupped the bowl of the wine glass; her attention was drowned in the liquid.

"What's with you?" I said.

"It's nothing." She took a sip and made a face while swallowing, as if an oversized capsule was stuck in her throat. "I saw a cat in the birch today."

"Well, you're acting like it was a bear," I said, then I turned the conversation back to Drew's promising problem solving. He's probably all the way in the concrete operational stage. And maybe it runs in the family, my family of course; maybe Skip's also got a little Mensa brain in there too.

Martha was still elsewhere.

I threw away the last of the plate, and sat beside her on the couch. "So you saw a cat in the leaner, Martha, big whoop."

She shrugged.

Then I put two and two together. "You think that explains the dead birds?"

"Makes sense to me."

"That would be some hunter," I said. "Eleven birds."

"Eighteen."

I pretended to strangle her.

"*At least* eighteen birds," she said. "God knows what else."

o o o

Only Shannon Doyle is dumb enough to sneak up on Drew when he's holding a chainsaw and cover his goggles with her hands. Skip stops splitting logs and turns around when he hears the saw shut off.

"Guess who?" she says, probably for the second time, while chewing gum. She's the clueless girl who gets killed in horror movies, but only after showing her breasts. Her parents are soap white — they live on the even whiter side of town — but she's camel coloured, with full lips and a full booty. Everybody's got theories on her mother.

Drew smiles under her hands, one foot on a stump, chainsaw at his side — a cross between Leatherface and a friendly lumberjack. He lists a number of female names, deliberately wrong. At each one, Shannon pouts, whines out a musical *Nooo*, and bends her knees, which sets off a jigglefest.

"I give up," he says.

Shannon vibrates her fists near her face in excitement and stretches her arms out for a hug, shoulders almost touching her ears. Drew takes her in one arm, hangs his chin on her shoulder. The chainsaw comes dangerously close to her bare leg. When they let go, Skip notices a spot of black grease on her thigh. Or maybe it's a bruise.

"You're going blonde." She vogues around Drew's fashionably dishevelled hair with both hands.

"It's the sun."

Their mother has been streaking Drew's hair in the summer since he was thirteen.

"Hi Skip!" Shannon's pitch rises, as if speaking to a child or someone with a disability. She bends over with her hands clasped between her thighs. She's taller than he is, but not that much. "You still at St. Jude's?"

"I'm a senior," Skip says.

"He's finishing a year early," Drew adds.

"Good for you!" An exclamation mark follows everything Shannon says. "How'd you do it?"

Skip shrugs. "I guess you have to sacrifice a lot."

Drew karate chops a V over his pelvis.

"You're so bad," Shannon says, flapping a hand at him. She resumes her hunched talking-to-a-three-year-old stance. "I'm sure your parents are very proud of you."

Skip rattles the maul over his head as if warding off a jinx. He could bring it down right through her upper back, split her head into perfect hollow halves like a coconut. Sacrifice. He's at the age where he plays betting games with himself like who's a virgin and who's gay. The row ahead of him in Chemistry, guys at the skate park, girls on the softball team. Shannon Doyle: definitely, definitely not sacrifice material.

She straightens up. She shoots Drew an inside look as if Skip were furnishing evidence for a previous charge laid against him.

"Dude," Drew says. He sounds like himself. "You're creeping us out."

The maul is still raised over Skip's head. But, to his credit, he isn't staring at Shannon's breasts.

Drew takes one of Shannon's hands and swings it in a wide arc while looking down at her. She does a little twirl — the extensions, the Monroe ring over her lip, the flip-flops, the cheerleader skirt, the infamous *derriere.*

"Damn, girl," Drew says.

She beams. Skip cannot figure out what they are to each other. Just friends, more than friends, bodies, jokes, good times, nothing? All this is complicated by the fact that Drew has a girlfriend in Albany he's serious about; Skip has seen her in the background of their webcam conversations, when he and Drew still used to do that.

"So can I see you guys cut something?" Shannon says.

They decide to fell the second of their quota of trees, right next to the one they did earlier that morning.

"Stand back here," Skip tells her. Who wears flip-flops to the forest? "You don't want to get hurt."

"She's fine," Drew says, "The lay's by the path, not this way." He spreads his legs to get a wider base and starts up the saw. First he makes the face cut at knee height, then the wedge cut, and finally the back cut from the other side of the trunk. The tree falls in slow motion, thunders when it bounces once on the ground. Drew walks to the fork of the tree and starts dividing a thick branch into foot-long rounds. It looks like a wiener cut into disks.

"You want to cut a round?" Drew says to Shannon.

She shakes her head and takes a step back. She wasn't afraid a few minutes ago.

"It's not as bad as it looks."

"Drew," Skip says. "If she doesn't want to, don't force her."

"Come on over here." Drew holds out a hand to her, as if coaxing a kitten. "Easy now."

Shannon takes high-kneed, flat-footed steps in her flip-flops.

"Really, Drew, we shouldn't mess around. We have a lot more to do."

"That's a good girl."

He settles behind her as if they're grinding at a club. He pulls the chain. She giggles.

"Drew," Skip says. He looks at Shannon's manicured toenails.

The cat came up again while Martha and I unwound with wine and cake after dinner. We almost never put the kids to sleep ourselves.

"That cat," Martha said, "spends all afternoon in the leaner."

"I've never noticed it."

"Well it does," she snapped as if I were doubting her. "Why are you always so — ugh."

I slivered another piece of cake for myself. If I didn't make a big deal, I figured Martha wouldn't notice.

"Any more dead birds?" I said to keep her attention off what I was doing.

"A couple right near the birch, right under the — Alan, you're making a mess." She took the knife from me and cleaned up the edge that I cut, widening the wedge of cake I was to get.

"Have you actually seen the cat kill anything?"

"No, but I'm sure of it." Martha said. "It has to be the cat. It slinks around for a while, then it stares me down when it hears me, then it gets this contented look on its cat face, because it thinks I'm a woman and I won't do anything."

"Do you hear yourself?"

"You think I'm lying? It gets this evil grin on its face because it's getting away with murder and it doesn't think a woman can do anything."

"The cat's male?"

"Yes."

"You've seen between its legs?"

"No, but it is."

"Martha, give it up."

"You give it up." She hovered over me and my cake. "Why can't you believe me? You've never seen it. You just said so yourself."

I put my palms up. Fine. If she wanted the cat to be male, so be it. She cupped one hand under the lip of the table, and swept crumbs into her palm.

Martha started again. "The cat sleeps all afternoon in the leaner. It must kill the birds in the morning, then — I don't think it eats the birds. It just kills them."

"It's a predator. That's what cats do."

"It kills birds," she said more forcefully, as if by repeating it she could transmit some obvious but still unknown point to me.

"So?"

"For sport, not for food."

"You want to domesticate it? Is that it?" I still wasn't sure where she was going. "It probably belongs to someone already."

She dusted the crumbs into the sink and placed the knife on the edge, so it balanced over the rim.

"I want you to kill it."

o o o

"I'll never do that again," Shannon says.

"You handled your business, boo."

"But I was *so* scared."

Drew and Shannon go on like this while Skip studies them. At one point, Shannon inspects her acrylic nails and actually says, *I think I chipped a nail,* and Drew takes her finger close to his face, rubs a fingertip along the curve of her nail, and says *Nah.* That's enough for her to believe she hasn't.

The felling, splitting, and stacking have been slow since Shannon's arrival. Skip and Drew are both splitting now, so that Shannon won't have to talk over the chainsaw. They take turns loading the wheelbarrow and transporting the firewood to a pile near the house. They'll stack them neatly along the garage, bark facing up, when she's gone. Shannon doesn't have much to say to Skip when Drew's off hauling a load. She concentrates on chewing her gum and pulling the ends of her hair hand over hand.

Drew announces a break. It's past noon.

"You want something to eat?" Skip says to Shannon. He's thinking a cookie, a Halloween-sized bag of chips.

"I guess." From her tone, Skip can tell she has a complicated relationship with food.

Skip looks at Drew. Same question.

"Just make me a couple of sandwiches. Ham."

"Can I have a salad then?" Shannon's eyes widen. Drew has raised the level of the menu.

"I don't think we have stuff for salad," Skip says. "You want an apple?" He stops himself from offering her ice cubes. Apparently, they're both bailing on making their own lunches.

"Yay, we could have a picnic," Shannon says and looks to Drew.

Skip raises his shoulders and squeezes his fists in mock excitement, the way Shannon did when she arrived. Neither of the others sees him.

Drew offers to show Shannon the conservation land at the edge of their property. "You'll love it."

"Can I wear these shoes?"

Drew turns his back to her and crouches. Shannon hops on for a piggyback, yelping and ducking under branches as they set off, her pleated skirt riding up.

o o o

The power went off after dinner, while my father was getting the boys ready for bed. Skip started crying from his crib, and Drew, who must have been brushing his teeth alone, called out for us.

In front of me, feeling her way up the stairs, Martha said, "What's the difference between killing a rat and killing a cat?"

She posed the question like a joke, so I waited for the answer.

"It's a real question," she said. "*I* don't see much."

Drew called out again. The toothpaste must have been burning his mouth.

"We're animals too, you know," I said. "What's the difference between killing a cat and killing a kid?"

"Nobody's killing kids, Alan. The kids can bloody well kill themselves. We were given dominion over all the beasts of the field."

"You're unbelievable." I laughed. We were groping our way down the hallway to the bathroom. "You of all people quoting scripture."

"What do you mean *of all people?*"

Then the electricity flickered on again. It didn't seem to be a conversation we could have in the light. Not with the fridge humming downstairs. Not with Drew on his step stool, holding his toothbrush over his shoulder like a weapon.

0 0 0

Skip decides to embrace the picnic idea. He washes fruit, prepares sandwiches, gets a clean blanket from the linen closet, then returns to the spot in the forest.

Drew and Shannon still aren't back.

Skip surveys the work accomplished in the morning versus the work left to do — a 30:70 ratio. After waiting five minutes, he sits on a corner of the blanket and starts eating. The wind irritates the leaves and squares of paper towel. A beetle advances toward the banana bread. Skip is starting his second sandwich when Drew and Shannon return.

"What's all this?" Drew says.

"The picnic."

"Picnic? You a fag or something?"

"It was Shannon's idea." Skip bobbles his head to remind Drew.

Shannon arrives a few paces behind Drew, swatting thin branches out of her face. She stands on a corner of the blanket and exhales a long tired *phhh*. She seems unsurprised by the spread of food, by Skip sitting on a blanket next to a chainsaw, eating a crustless sandwich. They are all Smurfs. The food must have sprouted from the forest.

"What did you think of the conservation?" Skip asks.

"The what?" She smoothes her clothes. "You mean the pond? There's this cool white tree over there."

Skip's chewing slows to a stop when he realizes where they went.

"Do you mind if I use your bathroom real quick?" Shannon says.

They shake their heads. As she walks away, her shirt rides up and Skip notices a tattoo in the middle of her lower back — an *A*.

When she's out of ear shot, he says, "You took her to the birch?"

Drew uses a paper towel to grab a sandwich. He smiles as he bites in. His answer.

o o o

One day I came home early so Martha could lead me into the forest and show me the cat. It was that important to her. I noticed that she had taped up the leaning birch, although we had not come to any agreement. The cat, when it saw us approaching, jumped from the horizontal stroke of the A up to a higher branch. Its orange coat camouflaged with the leaves.

I smiled and whistled at it.

"Don't bond with it," Martha said. "It's a killer." She was holding my arm with both her arms as we got nearer, torso and knees slack with fear.

"Don't go too close," she said.

I shook her off and approached the tree slowly. The cat followed me with its eyes. First I ripped off the silver tape from the trunk. The birch was *not* coming down. Then, with a broken branch, I reached up. The cat swiped at it gently, unable to grasp it.

"Kill it," Martha said behind me.

I looked back at her, surprised at how ridiculous she was being. "With what, Martha?"

The cat swiped more viciously this time, and Martha jumped back. She headed back to the house, gaining confidence as she moved further away from the cat.

Later, when I entered the kitchen, she was holding Skip flat against her chest. Without saying a word, I opened a can of tuna, breaking eye contact with her only to periodically check what I was doing. I pinched a morsel and threw it into my mouth. I even said *mmm* to irritate her. Then I went back to the birch and lured the cat down with a twig dipped in tuna.

o o o

Ashley, Angela, Andrea, Anna, Antoinette, Athena, Ariel, Amanda, Alice, Allison, Alana, Alan, Apple, Autumn, Adulteress, Able, Abel.

"You know she has an *A* on her back?"

"She showed me."

"For Andrew?"

Drew shrugs.

o o o

Over dinner, I thought Martha had flat out lost her mind. My father and I exchanged looks but he stayed out of it. She said something suggesting that I had betrayed her with the cat. I had yielded to its charms. That kind of melodrama.

I said point blank, "I'm not going to kill the cat."

"You don't care if it kills all the birds in New Hampshire?"

"I don't, no."

"It's got death coming." She ate a forkful of potato salad. "Just you wait and see." Another forkful. "Better say its prayers." Another forkful. "You live by the sword, you die by the sword." Then her mouth was too full to talk.

"I'm starting to worry about you," I said. "You want everything dead. The cat, the birch, the birds."

"Not the birds," she said.

"Pretty soon you'll be poisoning Dad's food — or mine."

She swallowed a lump and waved her fork. "How much is your insurance again?"

000

Shannon's approach is different from this morning. Whenever Skip looks across the lawn, she gets bigger incrementally, like a stick person on page corners being flipped. There's a tornado of leaves behind her.

It's her face that fills Skip with pity. The makeup, the Monroe ring, their purpose accomplished, now become excessive. The once proud vacancy of her face now has the abandoned look of a motel.

And Drew's different too, gentle words but rough tone, careful and careless with her, as if he couldn't hurt her more, but couldn't help her either. A father outside a delivery room.

Skip knows what happens at the birch. It's been happening since junior high. Their father, proud that the long-preserved *A* had become a tourist attraction, fanned Drew and his girls out the door toward the birch, which was not visible from the house.

What does he do with the condoms? Is there a used one in his pocket now?

The three of them eat in silence, mostly. Every once in a while a conversation flames up then dissolves, like fireworks.

Shannon doesn't seem to realize that she drove here and could leave any time. She's not even eating anything, Skip notices, just skinning a grape with her teeth. She's waiting for something from Drew.

"I was so scared when that tree fell," she says. "I thought it was like the end of the world."

"Ain't nothin'," Drew swallows a belch. "My mom says the whole house shakes."

The silence is creeping back, but Skip's determined to save this conversation.

"A tree falls in the forest," he says. "No one's around. Is there any sound?"

"Another tree fell?" Shannon asks Drew over Skip's head.

"You've never heard that?" Even Drew's incredulous. "Rewind brah."

"If a tree falls in the forest and no one's around, is there any sound?"

"Oh, I know that one," Shannon says. "God would hear."

"Excluding God." Drew takes over Skip's part. "Say God falls in heaven or goes deaf."

"The angels would hear."

"All right, same thing happens to the angels."

"The angels fell? But they fly. How can you fall if you fly?" She nibbles half the grape. "Still, we'd know if a tree fell. There'd be an earthquake like your mom said."

Drew gives up on the conversation. Skip too. They can hear the leaves tittering overhead.

A few moments later, Shannon says, "But one time my dad had a seizure at home and he was alone. I don't even remember. I was a kid. He said I was at school and Mom was out somewhere. And back then people didn't have cell phones. Can you imagine?" She chews the other half of her grape for a long time before swallowing.

"Is that all?" says Skip.

"Well yeah," she says. "Or no. When he came to, he couldn't like remember anything. He just knew he was on the floor and that everything looked different from down there. Like he was looking up the skirt of the world."

"We should get back to work," Drew says abruptly. He's up and walking toward the logs before Shannon's eyes focus again.

She combs her hair with her fingers, hand over hand. The background floods in: birds wanting to be noticed. *Chickawahwah. Wahwah.*

Skip can't find anything to say to cover for Drew. He holds out his hand. "You want your apple?"

000

Martha was wearing a broad-brimmed straw hat, which she tied under her chin in a bow. It had two cloth birds sitting on the brim. I called her my damsel whenever she wore it. We had decided to plant dusty millers along the driveway, because we got them on clearance, and because Martha thought they would be perfect to let guests know they had reached our house from the road. It was either that or a wrought iron gate with our initials welded into the pattern. We bought twenty, ten for each side. They'd look like runway lights when we were through.

I was digging a hole near the road, my back to Martha, when I heard her scream. The cat. It had attacked her from behind. One of its claws was still hooked in her hat so that Martha had to jerk her head to free herself. The cat leapt again, this time from in front of her. In the air, its body elongated to twice its length. Martha was sitting on her heels now, protecting herself with her hands, her back almost touching the ground. The cat carved two stripes in her forehead. She slapped her hands over her eyes and cried out again.

I blocked the cat with my leg as it was preparing to jump. Then I hit it with the back of the shovel. It hissed.

"Oh God," Martha said. Her hat was hanging around her neck.

I struck the cat again.

"Oh God! Oh God!"

Again.

Martha got up and ran toward the house, her forearm on her forehead, the other arm extended behind her as if she were pushing the scene away.

Again. Again. Again. Then I lifted the shovel high over my head, and brought the edge down on the cat's neck.

0 0 0

With Shannon gone, Skip's all business with Drew. His disappointment's keen. He doesn't care if he comes across as prissy. In a transparent effort to bond, Drew starts mocking Shannon, repeating what she said with a Valley girl accent. "My da-ad was like home alone, aaand he was on the flo-oor."

Skip doesn't find it funny. "She might not be the sharpest tool in the shed, but she really likes you."

Drew turns on him and lisps: "She might not be the sharpeth tool in the shed, but she really likth you."

"Loser."

Drew adds the wrists, and double slaps Skip on every *s*. "You have to thacrifith if you wanna be thmart like me."

"Don't hit me."

"Here'th your apple."

"I said stop it, Drew."

"I thaid thtop it." He adds the expressive eyes. "If a tree fallth in the foreth, ith there any thound?"

"You're a jerk."

Straight. "And you're a pussy."

Later that afternoon, before their parents come home, they walk deeper into the forest to take care of the last tree. Skip leads. His brother's eyes heat the back of his neck.

ACKNOWLEDGEMENTS

I am grateful to the Palazzo Rinaldi Artists' Residence in Italy, the Vermont Studio Center, and the Kimmel Harding Nelson Center for the Arts for residencies that enabled the completion of this manuscript. Thank you to Kwon Hyuk Moon, Oh Mi Il, Nancy Kang, and Patrick Cuff. Some of these stories appeared previously in *The Dalhousie Review, Descant,* and *The Madison Review.* This book would not exist without Freehand Books, so thank you to Sarah Ivany for her airtight production, Natalie Olsen for her design work, and a special thank you to Robyn Read whose insight has made each story here — and me — better.

Sentencing for the sections of "Criminal Activity" is taken respectively from sections 235 and 282 of the Criminal Code of Canada (R.S., 1985, c. c-46) and section 4 of the Controlled Drugs and Substances Act (1996, c. 19). Statistics for "Statistics" are taken from the United States Census Bureau, Statistics Canada, and the National Center for Health Statistics. The second section, *"is liable to imprisonment for a term not exceeding ten years,"* embeds a passage from T.S. Eliot's "The Love Song of J. Alfred Prufrock."

IAN WILLIAMS is the author of *You Know Who You Are* (poems, Wolsak and Wynn, 2010). *Not Anyone's Anything* is his first collection of fiction. He received his Ph.D. from the University of Toronto and is currently a professor at Fitchburg State University. He has held fellowships and residencies at the Vermont Studio Center, the Cave Canem, the Kimmel Harding Nelson Center for the Arts, and the Palazzo Rinaldi Artists' Residence in Italy. He divides his time between Ontario and Massachusetts.

¶ THIS BOOK WAS SET IN ALDUS BY HERMANN ZAPF
AND KNOCKOUT BY HOEFLER & FRERE-JONES.